ALTERED BRAND

J. Jay Myers

Walker and Company
New York

First published in the United States of America in 1993 by Walker
Publishing Company, Inc.

Published simultaneously in Canada by Thomas Allen & Son Canada,
Limited, Markham, Ontario

Library of Congress Cataloging-in-Publication Data
Myers, J. Jay.
Altered brand / J. Jay Myers.
p. cm.
ISBN 0-8027-1271-1
I. Title.
PS3563.Y397A79   1993
813'.54—dc20   92-45715
CIP

Printed in the United States of America

2 4 6 8 10 9 7 5 3 1

To Charlotte Will Myers—
valued critic, good wife, best friend

ALTERED BRAND

CHAPTER 1

THE TWO COWHANDS sitting on the veranda of the hotel watched the dude step off the stage in Yucca, New Mexico Territory. They had no way of knowing why he was there or that he was absolutely determined to succeed on his mission, no matter the danger or hardship. He was wearing steel-rimmed spectacles, a gray bowler, a well-tailored light gray suit, a white high-collared shirt, and an expensive black cravat. His face was youthful but city-pale. The idlers didn't notice the firm jaw, the solid shoulders, the flat belly, and the steel blue eyes. They laughed at him, but the two young saloon women passing by smiled and felt happier when the dude doffed his hat gallantly. In a most friendly but polite manner, he said, "Good morning, ladies."

Terrence Waddington Love heard the laughter and looked around to see where it was coming from. He had created the image he wanted. He smiled broadly and stepped up on the porch. "I guess you don't see many Easterners in Yucca. I'm T. W. Love and I'm going to be visiting a ranch near here for the summer." He offered his hand amiably to the nearest idler, a great mountain of a man who shook his hand and muttered his own name.

"Sorry, I didn't hear you," T. W. said.

"Oates. John Oates. Everybody calls me Big John."

"Glad to meet you, Big John."

"This here is Sundown. Shake hands, Sundown."

"Glad to meet you too, Sundown. Do you fellows know Jim Magruder? He's supposed to meet me here."

1

Big John asked, "You mean the Magruder that ramrods the JL spread?"

"If that means he's the foreman of the JL ranch, he's the one."

"Ain't seen him today. Sundown, you seen Magruder?"

"Nope, but I seen Wash Carter over at the Palace a little while ago."

Big John said, "He's a JL hand. Say, you ain't wearin' boots. And your shoes got buttons on 'em. Look at that, Sundown, buttons on his shoes."

"Don't that beat all?"

T. W., who did not like the name Terrence and wished his mother's maiden name—Waddington—was not part of his name, did not take offense easily. He was well aware of how uncommon his appearance must be to the two Westerners, so he smiled when he said, "You boys would be just as out of place in Boston, where I live." But there was a quality in his voice that stated plainly he had had enough of being mocked. Then he picked up his valise, made heavier by the books in it, and went to find the Palace and Wash Carter.

As he made his way along the boardwalk, T. W. carefully observed Yucca's main street. It was just six blocks long, and the side streets extended only a couple of blocks. It looked just like all the other Western towns he had passed through on the stage. Most of the stores and saloons featured square-shaped false fronts and most of them needed paint. There were a few adobe buildings scattered among the wooden ones.

But it was Saturday and the town was alive, full of cowhands and ranch families. T. W. knew people were looking him over and he heard the whispers and chuckles. Probably many of them had never seen a man dressed like he was. Eastern affectations had not yet reached the Estancia Valley, although during the stopover in Santa Fe he had seen businessmen wearing Eastern-style suits. He meant to buy range clothes as soon as he found this Wash Carter, but the impression he was making fit in perfectly with his mission. He wanted to be thought of as a harmless Eastern dude. That was one reason his Uncle Thad had sent him. Who would be afraid of a young Bostonian just graduated from Harvard who was poking around?

T. W.'s story was that he was spending the summer on his uncle's JL ranch, and that in the fall he was going back to Boston to begin his career with the Thaddeus Love Investment Corporation. It was true, but it was not the whole truth. Thad would have come himself, but there were important matters that would keep him in Boston for the next six months. Thad had said, "Anyway, Terry, you ought to have a summer in the West. You've spent a year on the deck of a China Trader. You've worked a summer as a Maine lumberjack. And you've spent a summer in France, England, and Italy. You need a summer on the open range. We've got investors thinking about putting money into beef cattle and ranches and you should know something about that business if you're going to advise them."

T. W. knew that Thad, the man who had been father and mother to him, would like nothing better than to be in New Mexico himself. He did come for a month most years and found it hard to return to Boston, but he had big responsibilities there. He often said, "Someday I'll chuck it all and go to the ranch and stay. Once you've come to love the high country with its mesas and mountains, you're never really happy anyplace else."

But all T. W. saw was an ugly town with a lot of unpainted buildings, a lot of people, and a lot of dust and horse manure in the street. He also saw the Adobe Palace saloon across that street and carefully picked his way through people, wagons, and horse apples. He pushed through the batwing doors and paused to allow his eyes to adjust to the semidarkness. It was cooler in the thick-walled adobe building and it was quiet. Saturday had not yet caught up with the Palace. There were only a few men at the long bar, and over in a corner some men were playing poker around a square table.

T. W. went up to the bar. A completely bald man with a big, black, well-trained handlebar mustache and an amused but friendly smile asked, "What'll you have?"

"Lemonade, please."

"Lemonade?"

"If you don't have that, I'll have a bottle of sarsaparilla."

"Don't have either one. Beer and whiskey is all we got."

"How about a glass of water? I just got off the stage and I'm really dry."

"Sure. Comin' up. Just in from Santa Fe?"

"Yes, but I don't live there. I'm from Boston and I'm on my way to the JL ranch if I can find a man named Wash Carter."

"He's right down there at the end of the bar," the barkeeper said, placing a glass of water on the bar.

"Thanks for the water."

Wash Carter, a black man, was leaning on the bar and staring up at a large painting of a nearly nude, generous-bosomed, wide-hipped, narrow-waisted reclining blond. She was wearing nothing except a rather diaphanous bit of drapery, strategically placed so as not to offend the more sensitive viewers—if there were any. Carter turned to T. W. and said, "Why are all these paintings of white women? There are plenty of black men out here in this country who'd like to see a good-lookin' black woman smilin' down from the wall. Doesn't seem right."

"Are you Mr. Carter?"

"That's what I answer to. Whole name's Washington Carter. Are you Terry Love?"

"Yes, but everybody calls me T. W."

"All right, T. W., I'm supposed to take you out to the JL. Didn't hear the stage come in. Sorry. Ready to go?"

"No, I want to buy a few things before I leave town."

"Some other clothes I'd guess. We'll go over to the Mercantile. Best clothes and best prices."

"I'll need your advice, Mr. Carter."

"T. W., do you mind if we don't 'Mister' each other? Hardly ever done out here."

"That's fine. It's just that I was taught not to use the first name of people older than I am."

"Well, I'm not that much older. Maybe ten years. So let's just forget those years. I'm Wash from now on."

Outside, T. W. could see that physically Carter was the kind of man he and his Harvard teammates had needed when they played the McGill University team in rugby. A rough game needed rough men and Carter was big in the shoulders, thick in the chest, and had thighs that strained his pant seams. And next fall Harvard was going to play Yale for the first time. How T. W. would like to play in that game, but his college days were over. He had no real regrets. He'd had a good time at Harvard, with rugby, boxing, and being editor of the *Crimson*. But he had not neglected his studies. He wasn't the best scholar, but he was near the top.

Now, all of a sudden, he was two thousand miles away, in a completely different world. It was a big tawny world with a clear blue sky and a bright sun, and it was full of people he didn't know. He was also playing a new game. He had to learn the rules and how to play the game, and he didn't have much time. His uncle was counting on him to uncover the reason why the JL had lost serious money the last two years, after many years of turning handsome profits. Somehow he had the feeling that this Wash Carter would help him, but he was less sure of Jim Magruder. Was Magruder dishonest or the victim of circumstances? Magruder had been the foreman in the ten profitable years prior to the last couple of bad ones.

"Wash, does the Mercantile sell rifles and revolvers?"

"They sell everything, from bustles to buffalo guns."

"I'll need your advice. I've used a rifle, but I've never had a revolver in my hand."

"Buyin' a six-shooter is one thing. Learnin' how to shoot it is something else."

The Mercantile was a big place and it had lots of Saturday customers. As they entered, Wash asked, "Know your sizes?"

"Yes."

"That'll save some time. Clothes are over here to the left."

A woman, with her back turned, was arranging some bolts of cloth on a counter.

"Miss Penelope, I brought you a new customer," Wash said.

Penelope Copeland turned around with a smile. "Hello, Wash."

She was strikingly beautiful. A mass of auburn hair was swept up above a face of perfect features and unblemished, creamy skin. Green eyes looked at T. W. for an instant as he sought for words that should have come easily. Then Penelope Copeland burst into a gale of laughter. She tried to say hello but she couldn't.

T. W. had never been laughed at by a woman. He was humiliated as people all over the store looked around to see what was going on. He became angry at her rudeness.

The young woman regained her composure and Wash said, "This is T. W. Love. He's visiting the JL this summer."

"How do you do," she said. "I'm so sorry. It's just that . . ."

Brusquely, T. W. said, "I know—that's why I'm here. I need some range clothes."

"I do apologize. I just was taken by surprise."

"Let's forget it and get on with our business."

Wash told T. W. what to get and T. W. gave the sizes.

Penelope brought the pants, shirts, and socks, and placed them on the counter.

"I'll need boots too."

Penelope asked what size and kind. She looked down at his feet and smiled at the sight of his button shoes.

Wash said, "Regular ridin' boots. Pointed toes, high heels, stitched, and knee-high."

After T. W. had bought a fawn-colored Stetson and a couple of red bandannas, he went to the back room and put on his new outfit.

He paid Miss Penelope Copeland and decided to gain a little revenge by leaving her a tip. When she realized what he had done, her eyes blazed and her face reddened. With a cold fury she said, "I do not accept tips, Mr. Love. I am part owner of this store."

"I *am* sorry. I should have realized that a lady of your impeccable manners would not be a mere employee. I apologize."

Then he said to Wash, "Let's go look at some firearms."

Penelope Copeland clenched her fists but did not think of a retort before T. W. walked away from the counter.

Wash accompanied him to the gun counter and said, "Miss Penelope and her father own the Mercantile and half the rest of the town. He's the mayor and she runs everything her father doesn't run. The church choir, the school committee, the dances, the box socials. Every white cowhand, rancher, and businessman has either asked her to marry him or wishes he had the guts to."

"I guess I shouldn't have insulted her but she really had it coming, Wash. Now how about a rifle and a revolver?"

"The newest six-shooter is this Colt. Called the Peacemaker. I just bought one myself. It's .45 caliber, feels good, and it's more accurate than most. For a rifle, I think you'll like the new Winchester .44-40. Fifteen shots and good power. Load it on Sunday and shoot it all week."

"Sounds good. I'll also need a cartridge belt, a holster, and some ammunition."

T. W. paid the clerk and started to strap on the belt and holster.

"You better think about whether you really want to do that," Wash said to him quietly.

"What do you mean?"

"Out here, people figure that if you're wearin' a gun you know how to use it."

"What do you mean by that?"

"Well, in the last few months there have been some men driftin' in here who get paid high wages, and they don't punch cows. They get better than top-hand money because their business is drawin' fast and not missin' when they shoot. We don't know who hires them, but they show up in town sometimes. A couple of harmless drunks have been gunned down for no more reason than bein' in the wrong saloon at the wrong time."

"How about the law?"

"We don't have a sheriff in Yucca. And Santa Fe is a good ride from here."

"Then there's really no law."

"There's a sayin' that the six-shooter is the law west of the Pecos. There's a lot of truth in it."

CHAPTER 2

WASH HAD ALREADY loaded the high-sided ranch wagon with some supplies and when Yucca had disappeared behind a ridge, T. W. asked, "How far out to the JL?"

" 'Bout ten miles."

"I've never seen land like this. Few trees. Just miles of sparse grass that grows in small bunches, a lot of what I think may be sagebrush and a lot of dirt. Does it ever rain?"

"Some. When it does, it comes quick and doesn't last long. Hardly ever have what you might call a rainy day."

After a couple of miles of silence, Wash said, "Know how to shoot a rifle?"

"I've hunted with Uncle Thad up in the Berkshires."

"Those mountains?"

"Nothing like these, but we call them mountains."

"Better get that Winchester out of the sack and load it."

"Sure, but why?"

"I just saw some pony tracks crossin' the road and those ponies weren't wearin' shoes."

"Indians?"

"Most likely. Comanches."

"Comanches are still hostile?"

"They're cattle rustlers and thieves and the best damn cavalry in the world. The army's been hard at work roundin' 'em up, but there's still a few around. These are the first ones I know of in months."

"All the people out here hate the Indians, I suppose."

"Just about."

"I've read some about the Indian problem. It seems to

9

me that they mainly are fighting to keep the white man from stealing their land. It's only natural to defend your homeland."

"I don't hate all Indians. Just the ones that steal JL cattle."

"Well, if the white man hadn't taken their land and the buffalo, they wouldn't need to be stealing cattle."

"I reckon you're right, but that doesn't make your uncle feel any better about not makin' a profit from the JL."

"Then you know about the losses."

"We all do. We figure that's why you're here."

"And I'm sure some are angry about my coming."

"Maybe Magruder. He thinks your uncle might not trust him and that hurts his feelins."

"How about the men?"

"They probably don't like it much. But they don't talk about it. I wish you would load your Winchester. We may need another rifle besides mine."

T. W. loaded the rifle, then said, "I don't see how anybody could ambush us. We can see for miles in every direction, and it must be twenty miles to the mountains on each side of us."

"This high country is rolling and a Comanche can suddenly appear at the next rise or out of an arroyo you don't know is there until it's too late."

"How many Indians might be in this group?"

"Only five or six, I think. They're probably just passin' through, but they might decide these two horses are worth takin' along."

"And a couple of scalps."

"Yeah, they might decide on that too."

A rifle shot split the afternoon's quiet and a bullet smashed into the side of the wagon. Wash shouted, "Get in back!" He stopped the frightened horses, tied the lines to the brake handle, and set the brake. He jumped down into the wagon. "Keep down. Don't take any chances. They won't shoot the horses because that's what they're after.

"You stay down, I'm gonna take a quick look. Yep, just what I thought. They're in that arroyo. If we show 'em we can shoot, they may go away. These two broncs ain't worth too much risk. But be careful about puttin' up your head. Some Comanches are real good with a rifle."

A bullet whined by and Wash slapped a shot toward the arroyo. "T. W., let's show 'em we've got two repeating rifles. It might make a difference. When I give the word, we'll both fire two shots, one right after the other. All right. Shoot!"

There was no answering fire and no Comanches appeared. Ten minutes passed, then T. W. said, "There's some dust about a half mile south."

"It might be a trick. We'll wait awhile."

"I'll replace the two cartridges."

"Good idea. I will after you do."

Soon Wash said, "All right, I'm goin' to have a look. Cover me."

He climbed out and carefully approached the arroyo. At the rim of the draw, Wash waved an all clear and returned to the wagon. "They decided it wasn't worth the chance against two with the new repeaters. Not good enough odds."

Neither man spoke as they rode along the narrow road. T. W. was thinking that he had probably passed the first test. He hadn't panicked, and Wash Carter could not know how fast his heart had been beating. Neither could he know how much T. W. Love was wishing he was back in Boston where the possibility of a violent death was quite remote.

T. W. suddenly wondered whether the attack was staged for his benefit, to make him think the JL losses were a result of Indian rustling. The attackers had left without much of a fight, almost suspiciously so.

T. W. asked, "You quite sure those were Comanches?"

"No, I'm just guessing."

"Could they have been white men?"

"With unshod ponies? Possible, but not likely. What's on your mind?"

"Well, I read the Comanches were all rounded up. Colonel Miles, Colonel MacKenzie, General Buell, Colonel Davidson, and Colonel Price came at them from all directions. Even Quanah Parker is on a reservation."

"That's pretty much the case from what I know, but Indians are contrary. They don't all do what their chief wants them to do. Of course those we just tangled with might even be on their way to a reservation. A couple of horses wouldn't hurt them any—for honor, and trading."

Maybe, T. W. thought. Maybe not. It was a slick answer and given quickly. He wanted to trust this Carter, but he couldn't be sure yet. He wasn't here to make friends. He was here to uncover misfeasance or malfeasance, if anything like that was going on.

They topped a rise and Carter said, "There's headquarters."

"There are trees. Looks more civilized."

"They're big old cottonwoods."

Headquarters was a long, rambling adobe house, an adobe bunkhouse, a big wooden barn, two corrals, a windmill, and a large watering tank. There was no clutter, everything was in its place. Thad Love's JL ranch was no shoestring outfit, and T. W. had known it would be first-class.

"Take your things on up to the house. The boys are all off working someplace but I guess Magruder will be in his office figurin' accounts. It's the end of the month."

T. W. stepped into a long hall. Seeing no one, he called, "Hello."

A man came out of a door and said, "Welcome. You must be Terry Love. Leave your luggage there, I'll have

Chin take it to your room later. Come on into the big room and we'll get acquainted."

"I'm pleased to meet you, Mr. Magruder. I've sure heard Uncle Thad talk about you a lot. I feel like I know you already."

Magruder had a firm handshake, and T. W. hoped it was a good sign. He also had a strong jaw, a shock of iron-gray hair, a wind- and sun-tanned face beneath the line where his hat usually sat. He was tall and lanky and walked with a slight limp. His eyes were brown and he looked directly at T. W. when he talked.

Magruder said, "This is your uncle's favorite room. He sits in here every night and reads."

T. W. could feel his uncle in the big room. There was a massive rock fireplace at one end, several large leather upholstered chairs, a bearskin rug in front of the hearth, some Navajo weavings on the walls, a mounted Big Horn sheep head on one wall and a large bookcase full of books.

"Tell me about your trip, Terry."

"Not much to tell, Mr. Magruder. And everybody calls me T. W."

"All right, T. W. it is then. And everybody calls me Jim. So how was your trip? Any trouble?"

"No trouble. Unless riding five days on a stage is trouble."

"I've never done that, but I've heard other people tell about it. The railroad should be in Santa Fe in a few years and it'll make a great difference to this valley. How's your uncle these days?"

"He's healthy and very busy. He may not get out here this year and that will make him very unhappy. He keeps threatening to give up all his responsibilities and come here to stay. And someday he just may do it."

"I know it's hard for him to leave here. This high valley is different from anyplace else. It gets inside of you and it never goes away."

T. W. told Magruder about the ambush and he seemed genuinely surprised. He said, "Thought they were all pushed over into Indian Territory. We've lost a lot of cattle and some horses to those devils the last two years."

"So they steal more cattle than they can eat?"

"Sure do. They've got a system, in cahoots with some white men. The Indians rustle the cows and drive them over the mountains to the Pecos, where they sell them to the whites we call Comancheros. Those bustards buy a few hundred head for a couple quarts of whiskey, and some trade goods for the squaws. They make a huge profit."

"So you believe if the Indians were really all rounded up, the rustling would stop."

"If and when they are. But the Comancheros aren't going to let a good thing die if they can help it. They only need five or six Comanches to gather those longhorns and drive them to the Pecos."

"Well, Jim, I don't know anything about ranching, but I'm here to learn all I can in a couple of months."

Magruder's expression abruptly changed from friendly to cautious and his eyes seemed to bore into T. W.'s. "That mean you want to examine the accounts?"

"No, Jim, I get enough of that from the reports you send to Boston. I'm here to learn as much as I can about the everyday operations of the JL. Uncle Thad says there are some big foreign investors who want to invest in cattle and ranches and I should know something about it all so I can talk to them without appearing too ignorant. I want to ride with the hands, learn to rope, brand, herd cattle. I want to be a cowhand for the next two months."

"Ever ridden a horse?"

"Not like these, but I have ridden. And I've done some fox hunting in Virginia. But I know nothing about this ranching business."

"Well, what I'd better do, T. W., is have Wash Carter be

your teacher. He's the best man I have. When I retire, I'm going to recommend him to be the next JL foreman."

"Are you seriously thinking about retiring?"

"Not immediately. But when a man gets to my age he gets to thinkin' seriously about it and tries to pick the right time. I've saved enough to do it. Maybe this year or maybe next year. Depends on a number of things. But I'll give Thad fair warning."

"Wash Carter appears to be a solid, reliable man. Can you spare him?"

"We have a little slack time right now, until hayin' starts."

"How about the other employees, Jim?"

"We have a good crew. All of them been here for at least two years. A few of them five or six. They're good hands and they're loyal to the brand."

"And Chin?"

"Best cook in New Mexico Territory. He's one reason we keep our men so long. Your uncle gave him a job years ago when he needed one and he feels indebted. Other outfits have tried to hire him away from the JL but I doubt he'll ever leave. At least not as long as Thad is alive."

"Thanks for filling me in, Jim. I think I'll go out and look around. Get my bearings and see where things are."

"We'll eat in the bunkhouse if you don't mind. Easier for Chin. He's getting older, too. You'll hear him yelling in about an hour."

CHAPTER 3

IN THE MORNING T. W. met Wash at the corral, where the men were roping and saddling their horses. Some of the mustangs started the day with some halfhearted bucking. None of the men had ridden out yet when a tall, skinny, young redhead called Brick came over to Wash and T. W.

"You want me to catch one for you, T. W.?"

"I don't know how to throw a rope yet, Brick. So maybe you should."

"How about that bay gelding over there? He's not in anybody's string right now, but he's a good one."

"Fine. Looks strong."

"He can go all day."

Wash said, "I don't know about Sam. Nobody's ridden him for about a week. He's apt to be a bit salty."

"I'll try him, Wash."

Brick went to cut Sam out of the bunch. Wash took T. W. aside and said, "I think the boys are aimin' to have a little fun with you. But no matter what happens, don't grab the saddle horn. It's just not done."

When Brick tightened the cinch, Sam reared up straight. T. W. looked around at the men. They were not looking at him and they all wore poker faces. Still, no one had left. They were waiting to see the fun. T. W. pulled his new Stetson down tight, hitched up his pants, and walked over to where Brick was holding Sam. The big bay was skittering around. Brick handed the reins to T. W., but held on to the cheek strap until T. W. was in the saddle.

"Let him go!"

For an instant, Sam did not move, then he exploded

straight up. He landed stiff-legged, then started crow-hopping and sun-fishing. On the first quick twist to the left, T. W. lost the saddle and sailed off to the right. He landed hard but bounced up. The men were laughing. T. W. smiled and said, "Catch him again, will you, Brick?"

Twice more the horse deposited T. W. in the corral dirt. On the fourth attempt Sam did not buck much and T. W. stayed astride. He yelled, "Open the gate!" and the two streaked out in a cloud of dust. When they returned, T. W. slipped off and started to tie the reins to the gatepost.

Wash said, "You don't have to tie him. Just drop the reins and he'll stand there."

The men were already riding off and T. W. said to Wash, "That was really tough. I didn't do very well."

"You showed 'em two things—you don't know much about ridin' broncos . . . and you've got guts."

"Will Sam do that every morning?"

"Not that much. He'll settle down after a couple days. Several of these waddies have been thrown by Sam when he hadn't been worked for a while."

"I bet no one else was thrown three times in a row."

"No," Wash said and laughed. "Not three times in a row."

"Wash, I noticed all the men wear pistols and have rifles in their scabbards. You said no one should wear a gun unless he knows how to use it, so I guess they all know how."

"None of 'em are quick-draw artists. They wouldn't want to tangle with any of those rannies I told you about, but they can shoot some."

"I want to wear a gun with some feeling of confidence, so I'd certainly appreciate it if you show me what I ought to know."

After two hours of instruction and practice Wash said, "That's all I know. You just have to keep practicing. And be sure you clean that Peacemaker regularly or it'll get rusty in a hurry."

After dinner T. W. went behind the barn and shot a box of cartridges at a tin can—not very far away. Before he quit, he was hitting it almost as often as he missed. Then with an empty cylinder, he tried what he had read and heard about, a fast draw. After an hour of working at it, he was no faster than when he started.

Wash returned from a job he had taken care of and watched T. W. for a few minutes. He said, "If you want to be good at that, you'll have to spend most of the summer at it. You'll also have to wear your holster lower on your leg and tie it down with a leather thong. You want to do all that?"

"No, I probably don't. I was just experimenting. I can see the problems, and why you would have to spend so much time. I think you would have to stand in front of a mirror and analyze every part of the move to eliminate all the unnecessary motion."

"Most honest men out here don't have the time to do that, T. W. Usually it's just the crooks, the hired guns, and the lawmen who learn to draw fast and shoot straight. The rest of us just practice hitting what we shoot at. That is, when we have the money to buy the bullets. We spend our money on more pleasurable things, and bein' this close to Yucca, that's pretty easy to do."

The rest of the afternoon T. W. spent learning to handle a rope. He wanted to be able to catch his own horse as soon as possible. And he knew that if he wanted to be accepted by the men, he would have to be able to rope cattle. By the end of the day Wash said, "Tomorrow we'll try roping from the back of a horse."

The next morning, after the crew had left, T. W. tried to rope Sam, but Sam was used to the morning game and evaded the loop four times. On the fifth throw, T. W. caught him. Wash had to hold Sam while T. W. saddled and mounted him. The horse did not buck with as much enthusiasm as he had the day before, and T. W. hit the dirt only once. Then Wash explained the intricacies of roping from the saddle. There were two ways of attaching the rope to the saddle horn: tie the end of the rope to the horn before throwing the rope or "dally" it after throwing and catching the steer. Most New Mexico cowhands tied first. Wash said, "Less chance of losin' a couple fingers." T. W. became a "tie-man."

In a few days T. W. was out with Wash, riding the line, checking the condition of cattle in different parts of the JL, hazing cattle from overgrazed areas to new grass, and watching for those with screw worms. Wash taught him how to read sign, look for tracks of wolves, coyotes, cougars, and Indians. It was fascinating to the Harvard graduate. What would his friends in Boston think if they could see him? Especially now that his range clothes were not so new and his Stetson was dusty and showing sweat marks around the hat band.

T. W. began to find himself watching the fast-moving clouds that were so close overhead. He thought the sky was bluer than anywhere, except perhaps out over the Atlantic. The air was light and there was always a breeze. The sun was hot, but the air was cool and dry, and every night was a blanket night. The summer climate, at least, was better than any place he had ever been.

But after two weeks T. W. had not even a single clue about why the JL was losing money. There were no loafers. Every day's work was planned and organized. Magruder was no office foreman. He was out every day checking on grass and cattle and watering places. If he resented T. W.'s presence, he gave no evidence of it. No one had seen any Indian sign lately. Apparently no longhorns had been stolen for a month.

On T. W.'s third Saturday Magruder gave the crew the afternoon and night off. The men gave each other haircuts, took baths, shaved, and put on clean clothes. All of them strapped on their gunbelts.

T. W. asked, "Should I wear my Colt, Wash?"

"Up to you."

"Since I'm new around here, I'm just wondering if I might attract more attention with it or without it."

"Most people won't notice one way or another. But I'd say you're about as good with it as most of our men."

"Well, I think I can take care of myself without a gun."

The JL bunch galloped into Yucca in the best tradition— in a cloud of dust, and with some high-pitched whoops. They put their horses in the town corral and drifted off, each man with his own priorities. Brick and two others went to an imposing two-story white frame house. It was down at the end of the main street and set off by itself— the only building in town with a fresh coat of paint. There was a white picket fence, and even the hitching rack was white.

T. W. saw it and asked Wash, "Is that . . . ?"

"Yep, and it's the best in the Territory, includin' Santa Fe. Prentice Parlors is the name. Goldie usually has about ten lovelies. They're clean and pretty and pleasant. She doesn't water the drinks and she doesn't put up with rowdies or drunks."

"Looks fancy."

"It is. Carpets, drapes, nice furniture. Nothin's cheap, 'specially the prices."

"Wash, what's the position of these women in the community?"

"You mean, do they go around town like everybody else?"

"Yes."

"Four years ago some kind of plague swept through the town and people were awful sick. Some died. Goldie and her girls turned the Parlor into a kind of hospital and they were real good nurses. They took a big risk and some of 'em took sick, too. Folks appreciated it all. Lots of the wives have even accepted them to a certain extent."

"Maybe they figure Goldie's girls help make the town safer for them and their daughters."

"Sometimes Goldie sings in the church choir and a few of her girls attend services once in a while. I think Goldie just likes to sing, and that's her best chance."

"Wash, you're kidding an Eastern dude."

"It's the truth. She even advertises in the *Yucca Sentinel*. Has a few lines about any new girl and other events at the Parlor. And at the bottom of her ad she puts her slogan: 'Ask any man.' "

"I don't believe it."

"It's the truth. Remember, there aren't too many women out here. This isn't Boston."

"Does Goldie have any . . . uh . . . black girls?"

"Always has at least one or two. Tell you something else. Most of the Parlor girls only last a year or two because some lovesick rancher or puncher marries them."

"What a contrast with Boston."

"Let's drop in at the Palace, T. W. I could use a little redeye to cut the dust in my throat."

"I don't drink, Wash, but I'll go with you."

The Palace was alive. A tinny piano could be heard above the loud conversation and raucous laughing. A few Palace girls were dancing with cowhands. Others were sitting at tables with men who bought them watered drinks. The gamblers were playing either poker or monte. Wash and T. W. joined the customers standing at the long bar. Heinie, the bartender, came over and spoke to T. W. "Say, I bought a case of that sarsaparilla. I even drank a bottle myself. Ain't bad. Want some?"

"Sure do."

"The usual for you, Wash?"

"You bet."

As the two JL men drank they turned to watch the Palace action. Wash asked, "Play poker, T. W.?"

"Not much—and never with strangers."

"Smart man. Say, there's Big John over at the corner table."

"Big John Oates and his friend Sundown."

"How do you know those two?"

"They laughed at me when I got off the stage. I would guess they're kind of simple, and harmless."

"Right, except when Big John drinks too much. Which he seems to be doin' today."

"He's big, Wash."

"We humor him. But he gets pretty mean sometimes."

Just then Big John saw Wash and T. W. and yelled, "There's the dude. He's changed his clothes, but he's still a dude."

John and Sundown made their way through the crowd toward Wash and T. W. Oates was steady on his feet, but his eyes looked small and his face was flushed. He stopped in front of T. W. "Yep, once a dude, always a dude."

T. W. smiled. "I'll buy you a drink, Big John."

"I can't stomach that sweet, dude stuff you're drinkin'. Now if you wanna drink a man's drink, I'll drink with ya. Whadya say, dude?"

"Sorry, John, I'll buy you one, but I don't want one myself."

"Aw right, dude. I'll buy *you* a man's drink. Heinie, bring a couple o' whiskeys over here for me and the dude."

Wash said, "Don't push it, John. He doesn't want one."

"Stay out o' this, Carter. I'm askin' the dude to have a drink with me. Nobody turns me down. It ain't friendly, and I don't like people who ain't friendly. Don't like 'em at all."

Big John stepped back and pulled out his six-shooter. Suddenly the Palace was silent. Wash said, "Put that iron back in the holster, Oates. T. W. isn't wearin' a gun."

"I know he ain't wearin' a gun. I don't aim to shoot him much either. Probably not at all." Then he looked at T. W. "If you won't drink with me, you can entertain me and the rest of the folks."

T. W. spoke slowly and carefully. "I don't sing or dance. Put your gun in your holster and I'll buy you a drink of the best stuff in the house."

"You can do a little jig. Everybody can do a jig," Oates said, pointing his gun at T. W.'s feet. "Jig, dude."

Wash started toward John, "Put that away. Now!"

T. W. said, "Wait, Wash. Maybe I can do a little Irish jig. I'll take off my glasses and put them here on the bar."

He took a step from the bar and suddenly erupted into action. He shot his left foot out and kicked John's gun hand. The pistol landed ten feet away and John cursed and shook his hand with the pain and surprise. T. W. stepped in and sank a hard left into John's belly. He stepped back, into the classic boxing stance he had learned in his college boxing-team days. John roared and rushed forward. T. W. danced aside and landed a hard right on Oates's ear as he went past. Infuriated, John roared again and came back slowly with his arms wide, hoping to get in close for some old-fashioned rough-and-tumble action. But T. W. stepped in quickly with a left jab and a right cross to the jaw, then danced away.

Big John tried to force T. W. back against the bar where he couldn't get away. T. W. waited for him, then moved in with a flurry of blows to the face that snapped John's head back and opened a cut above his right eye. Then he circled away from the bar and slipped in again and again with lightning punches that befuddled Big John.

T. W. went to work on John's belly and when John brought his arms down to protect himself, T. W. beat a tattoo on his face. The boxing coach had always said, *Get the belly and the head will follow.*

Big John was swinging wildly and hitting nothing. He

was getting a fine lesson in the art of boxing. Both eyes were swelling. Blood from his cut flowed into his right eye. Blood streamed from his nose, but still he came on, still trying to attack. T. W. started to move inside again but he slipped on the sawdust-covered floor just as John started a wild, looping right. His fist caught T. W. on the side of the head. Bursts of light exploded in T. W.'s head as he went down. But he knew he had to get up. Big John might kick him in the head or the ribs. He forced himself to his feet. He had to stay away until his vision cleared. John couldn't catch him and finally yelled, "Come on and fight like a man. Stop dancin' like a girl."

T. W. knew John's big punch had slowed him. He could now be hit again and the next one might be the end. He had to put John away quickly. He moved toward him slowly as if he were going to take up the big man's challenge. He invited another roundhouse right, and when John started it, T. W. stepped in with a left deep into the belly. As the head came down, he measured Big John, and hit him with a short, chopping right exactly on the magic button of the chin. Big John's knees buckled and his massive hulk collapsed into the sawdust.

The yelling and whooping that had filled the Palace stopped. Big John Oates lay helpless on the floor. And he had been put there by a man who weighed a hundred pounds less than he did. Wash Carter stood at the bar with his hand on his partly drawn gun, keeping an eye on the crowd. T. W. moved to Wash's side.

"What'll happen now, Wash?"

"I don't think anything will. It was a fair fight."

Wash went over and picked up John's pistol. He handed it to Sundown. "Better keep this for him until we see what he's like when he comes out of it."

T. W. said, "Maybe I can drink my sarsaparilla now." And he turned his back to Big John and the friends who had gathered around his unconscious bulk.

Wash stood sideways so he could see whatever happened next. He said, "He's startin' to move a little. You want to get out of here?"

"No. If there's going to be more trouble, it might as well be now."

"They're helping him up. His face is sure a mess. He's comin' over here."

T. W. turned and faced Big John. He tensed his muscles and put his weight forward on the balls of his feet, ready to move in any direction. John stopped in front of him, hooked his thumbs in his gunbelt, and looked T. W. over from head to foot.

"That's the first time in my life I was ever whipped. But it was fair and square. What's your real name?"

"My friends call me T. W."

Big John turned to the crowd and said, "His real name is T. W., and if anybody calls him dude, he'll answer to me." Then he turned and walked out through the batwing doors.

T. W. exhaled a long breath and let his muscles relax. "Is that it, Wash?"

"Yeah, that's it. I'm sure. Like I said, he's only mean when he's real drunk. He'll probably even be friendly the next time you see him."

T. W. put on his spectacles and said, "I'm really near-sighted, Wash. It's a good thing he stayed in close."

Shorty and several JL hands came up. Shorty said, "You're the first one ever stood up to Big John. He's had everybody buffaloed for a long time. You'll do to ride the river with, T. W."

"Thanks, Shorty. But it really wasn't a fair fight. He was drunk and he doesn't know anything about boxing."

As Shorty and the others went back to their poker game Shorty said, "That four-eyed maverick can sure enough hold up his end. And Sam ain't throwed him for a week now. He might make a pretty good hand even if he is a college boy."

The piano player began to play and one of the girls began to sing a ballad. The poker games and the drinking settled back to normal. Wash said, "Let's sit at a table and watch the people."

"Yes, I've had enough excitement for a while."

As they picked up their drinks, Heinie said, "Hear what happened over on the Pecos?"

Wash said, "No, what?"

"It's here in the Santa Fe paper." And Heinie handed *The New Mexican* to Wash.

CHAPTER 4

WASH SAID, "LISTEN to this, T. W. 'A report is in circulation that a party of Comancheros were attacked over on the Pecos by a band of Texans. All Comancheros were killed. The report comes in a roundabout way, but credit is given it because the source is a reliable one.'"

"It sounds like you were right, Wash. They were still operating."

"Here's another article. 'A few days ago a party of Comanches made a raid on Mr. Maxwell's herd and ran off several hundred head. A party of men overtook them and hung them all.'"

"Where's Maxwell's ranch?"

"Over on the Pecos and south from here. One of the biggest in the Territory, so he had plenty of hands to send after them."

"Then this might end the rustling."

"Might slow it up some. For a while."

"Or, I suppose, it just might make the rest more careful."

The two men sat with their drinks and watched the Palace action. But the two articles were bothering T. W. Citizens in both cases had taken the law into their own hands. Perhaps innocent men had been killed. Or, even if those men were guilty, the next instance of that kind might see innocent men killed. Also, T. W. was asking himself whether men should die for stealing cattle. It wasn't such a heinous crime. He knew the Easterner was questioning the Westerner's sense of justice, but he believed that in both cases the wrongdoers should have been apprehended and brought to trial.

"Wash, doesn't anything disturb you about those two articles?"

"No. They're both pretty good news, it seems to me."

"We don't know that those men who were killed were guilty."

"We don't know it, but if a man isn't a Comanchero, he shouldn't be keepin' company with 'em and actin' like 'em."

"That's guilt by association, and that's a dangerous philosophy. An innocent man might have been with them because he didn't know what they were, or they may have been holding him against his will."

"T. W., both of those situations are possible, but not likely. Usually there isn't time to find out those things."

"You approve, then?"

"The law out here is usually a long way from where a crime is committed."

"Couldn't the alleged criminals be captured and taken to where the law is?"

"That's not as easy as you make it sound. A lot of things can happen takin' some prisoners from the Pecos to Santa Fe."

"Well, I don't think death is a proper punishment for stealing cattle."

"It may not be proper, but it's what happens out here, and every rustler knows the chance he's takin'."

"Do you ever wonder how a man might have gotten into a position where he does that?"

"I know, one wrong turn in his life and before he knows it he can't get out of the spot he's in. He can't ever go back and start over."

"Exactly."

"I've thought about it. I saw three young rustlers swing from a cottonwood over in Chavez, and I wondered. But,

T. W., if rustlers weren't strung up, nobody's herd would be safe. It's just the way it has to be. Out here, if you don't personally protect what's yours, you're looked on as not much of a man. And that makes you fair game for any Comanchero or any cowhand who's tryin' to increase his herd the quick way."

"That's the job of the law."

"Look, when Big John got out of hand, you didn't call for the law. You took care of him yourself. You protected yourself."

"Yes, Wash, but I didn't kill him. He's still alive. Did you ever kill a man?"

"Too many. I was in Sherman's army, at Nashville—and other places."

"Were you from Tennessee?"

"Born and raised a slave. After the war I was in the Tenth Cavalry under Colonel Benjamin Grierson. We fought Comanches and Kiowas, and I was at Fort Sill when Satanta, Big Tree, and Satank surrendered."

"If it's not too personal, why did you leave the army?"

"I was tired of army life and I figured I could make more than thirteen dollars a month."

"You've been with the JL for a while?"

"Five years. Magruder not only gave me my first job, he taught me what I know about cows and ranchin'. I owe him a lot, and if you're thinkin' he's not honest, I'm sure you're barkin' up the wrong tree."

"He seems honest, Wash, but I've got to find out why the JL is losing steers and money. I can't leave any stone unturned."

"Speakin' of steers and money, Britt MacKenzie just came in. He's at the bar. Biggest man there."

T. W. looked at the tall man, heavy in the chest and shoulders, with black wavy hair showing beneath his pushed-back silver-belly Stetson. He was wearing well-tailored ranch clothes. "He looks like money, Wash."

"He owns the Pothook spread north of the JL. His herd has grown so fast that Magruder and I wonder what he feeds his cows to make 'em have so many calves."

"You think he might be rustling JL cows?"

"Maybe. But not many others do. He's a close friend of the Copelands. He even comes into church most Sundays. Then he has dinner cooked by Miss Penelope herself. Most folks think the Mercantile and the Pothook will soon be mergin'."

"Is there any reason to suspect him, besides the fact that his herd is increasing so rapidly?"

"I think so. He talks too much about law and order. He says Yucca ought to have a sheriff and the valley ought to have a marshal."

"Maybe he's sincere."

"Maybe, but I don't trust a man who talks about it as much as he does, when everybody knows Yucca and the valley can't do that for a long time yet. He's been here three years. I don't know where he came from, but he had some money when he got here. Enough so he got a good loan from the bank."

"Has there ever been any trouble between the Pothook and the JL?"

"Britt was a little hot last year when his big black stallion was stolen and he thought one of our hands did it. He chased this man clear up into Colorado, caught him, and hung him on the spot. But we convinced him the horse thief was just a drifter who stayed the night at the JL."

"Another example of on-the-spot justice, Wash."

"Stealin' a man's horse is just as bad as murder out here. Britt did what every man would do if he could."

"I can't accept that kind of justice, not when it comes to taking someone's life."

"You may change your mind, T. W. You may have to."

"I guess time will tell. I'm going over to the Mercantile

to get some cartridges. Want to come along, or do you have plans?"

"I'll just sit here for a while. Might get in a friendly poker game pretty soon."

T. W. went to the Mercantile.

Penelope was up front arranging some bolts of cotton and she greeted him pleasantly. "Good afternoon, Mr. Love."

He noticed she seemed less standoffish than she had before. Suddenly, he felt a bit self-conscious. He wished he had stopped to clean up a little after the fight.

Penelope's interest in him was not at all thwarted by his slightly disheveled appearance. On the contrary. Because exciting news traveled fast in a town like Yucca, Penelope had already heard about the action at the Palace and she was impressed. She had found it hard to believe a man the size of T. W. could actually defeat a giant like Big John Oates, but when three different men rushed in to the Mercantile to announce the news, she had to accept it as truth. It was certainly amazing and she was quickly wishing she knew more about the nephew of Thad Love.

It was true he pronounced some words in a peculiar way and some people mocked his accent when they spoke about him. She had tried not to laugh when they did that. She knew it wasn't fair and she knew a good churchgoing woman shouldn't laugh when someone ridiculed another, but some of the men had his accent down pat. Up until now, most of the men she had heard mention him thought he was a sissy as well as a dude. She and he had certainly gotten off to a bad start when he had come in to outfit himself for his summer at the JL, but there was obviously much more to him than she had thought then.

"Good afternoon," T. W. said. "I see the Mercantile is busy today."

"Saturdays are our busiest days. I just heard that Big John Oates finally met his match."

"It wasn't much of an encounter."

"You're too modest. Not even Britt MacKenzie has taken such a chance."

T. W. pretended not to have heard the name before. "Britt MacKenzie?"

"Yes, he's John's employer, on the Pothook ranch, and he's a staunch advocate of law and order."

"That is certainly to his credit. And I'm certain Mr. MacKenzie could do what I did if the need arose."

"Be that as it may, you are Yucca's hero today. By the way, I do hope you will attend the community dance tonight. Nearly everyone will be there. It would be an opportunity for you to meet the leaders in our town."

"An excellent idea. I imagine it is futile at this late date but I'll ask anyway. Will you do me the honor of accompanying me to the festivity?"

Penelope was surprised. She was accustomed to having everyone know she was keeping company with Britt MacKenzie. "I'm really sorry, but I have already accepted an invitation."

"Perhaps another time."

"I'll look forward to it."

He thought she had sounded sincere. What prompted him to ask her, anyway? Was it just that perverse streak in his nature? Maybe not. She was beautiful, and as well-groomed as any woman in Boston. She had that lovely auburn hair. She must have been to a good school somewhere because she spoke flawless English. And he had always been captivated by women with green eyes.

He bought his ammunition, and as he left the Mercantile he held the door open for a young woman with several packages. The pretty brunette walked along the boardwalk just ahead of him and he was admiring her small waist and the way she walked, when suddenly a dirty black-and-white cat dashed across the street with a barking hound in close pursuit. The woman stepped aside quickly and one of her packages fell to the boardwalk. T. W. sprang to the rescue, picked up her package, and said, "Hello again."

She said, "I'm sorry to trouble you, but thank you—again."

This young woman had light blue eyes, well-coiffed black hair, and a genuine smile. He immediately decided that she was the kind of person he could talk to for hours, about all kinds of topics. Although she was not strikingly beautiful like Penelope Copeland, this woman had a soft kind of beauty, and she was just as well-groomed as Penelope.

Doffing his hat, T. W. said, "My pleasure to be of service. My name is T. W. Love."

"Mine is Jennifer Prentice."

"Let me help you with these—the dog and cat might come tearing by again."

"You're very nice. Thank you."

As they started walking, Jennifer said, "I have heard your name several times this afternoon, Mr. Love."

"News does travel fast in Yucca. That fracas is best forgotten. I'm not really a brawler." T. W. saw that Jennifer was not wearing a wedding band and he felt very attracted to her. So he said, "I hope you will forgive me if this is too forward, but I have just learned there is a community dance tonight and I have just met you, so I could not have asked you before this moment. Will you do me the honor of accompanying me to the gala this evening?"

Jennifer was momentarily flustered as she seemed to search for the right words. "That's very nice . . . I . . . why, yes, I'm sure I can arrange things. Yes. I'd love to go with you, Mr. Love."

They walked along, exchanging small talk, which Jennifer did very easily. When she stopped walking she said, "This is where I live . . . with my sister. I'm looking forward to this evening."

T. W. gave her back her packages and said, "I am too. It

should all be very enjoyable. I'll call for you around seven-thirty."

He opened the white picket gate and watched her go up the walk to the large, freshly painted white house. All at once he realized that this was the house Wash had pointed out earlier—the one called Prentice Parlors, managed by Goldie Prentice. Jennifer was Goldie's sister. At first T. W. was stunned. Then he was amused. He knew what the reactions of his friends in Boston would be. They would be aghast. More importantly, what would his uncle's reaction be? Well, it would probably be what he had always said about going out with girls: Enjoy yourself with the lady and mind your manners.

When the silky, light blue, full-cut skirt disappeared inside the big door, T. W. turned and walked back to the Palace. Wash was sitting at a corner table playing poker, so T. W. bought another sarsaparilla and stood at the bar, just watching people and thinking. He tried placing his Boston friends in the Palace. They did not fit. They didn't fit anywhere in New Mexico. He knew that none of the Boston girls could cope with living in Yucca if they were suddenly thrust into it. Under desperate circumstances, they might resort to becoming employees of Goldie Prentice. Possibly, if they were stranded without any other resources . . . but no, he couldn't imagine any of them in that situation. They would be shocked if they knew what he was thinking at that moment.

Of course, he had been very surprised about Jennifer Prentice, for that matter. One of Thad Love's favorite sayings was never more true: You can't tell a book by its cover.

Wash left his poker game and joined T. W. at the bar. "What have you been up to?"

"Well, a very interesting thing has happened. I met a beautiful young woman and asked her to go to the dance.

She accepted and when I walked her home, I discovered she is Goldie Prentice's sister Jennifer."

Wash smiled broadly. "Remember what I told you. Most of Goldie's girls don't stay with her very long. Somebody marries them."

"Wash, seriously . . . is Jennifer . . . does she . . . just live with her sister?"

"She works in the Upper Parlor. Only the best work up there, and the price is high. She's been here about six months. She was only in the lower parlor a few weeks."

"She just doesn't seem like she would have that kind of a job."

"Not all painted up like the saloon girls? Not hard lookin'?"

"I guess so."

"I told you, Goldie's girls are high class. You still aim to take her to the dance?"

"I certainly do. Nobody will give her a hard time, from what you've told me?"

"People may be surprised that she isn't workin' on Saturday night, but nobody will want her thrown out, if that's what you're worried about. Like I told you, Goldie's girls are respected."

"Wash, I wonder if I will ever understand this New Mexico. Well, I'm going to the barbershop for a real bath, a shave, and a haircut. By the way, are you going to the dance?"

"I wouldn't miss this one. I want to see the faces of the Copelands and the other townsfolk when they see who Thad Love's nephew has brought to the dance."

CHAPTER 5

T. W. WALKED THROUGH the white picket gate and up to the door of Prentice Parlors. He admitted to himself that he felt self-conscious. It was certainly a new experience. He rang the bell and a tall black man in tailored gray trousers and a white shirt with a black string tie opened the door. He looked to be about Wash's age and had the same appearance of self-confidence and self-worth. He said, "Good evening. Right this way, sir."

"I'm T. W. Love. I've come to take Miss Jennifer to the dance."

"Make yourself comfortable here in the parlor. I'll tell her you're here."

T. W. sat down and looked about him in amazement. The room was done in simple elegance. No purple walls or such garish furnishings as he had expected. There was excellent taste in all of the appointments—coordinated in a French motif. A white marble fireplace was at one end of the room. On the mantel were two ornate, highly polished silver candelabra. The draperies were silk. The carpeting, upholstery, walls, and draperies were all in quiet tones of beige.

"Good evening, Mr. Love."

Coming through the doorway with a welcoming smile was a statuesque blond. She wore an evening gown, cut low and off the shoulders. It appeared that she had been molded into it in order to display every breathtaking physical charm. She seemed amused at T.W.'s awe, but she said very graciously, "Welcome. Jennifer will be down in a moment. I'm Goldie Prentice, her sister."

T. W. stood up, hoping his mouth had not been gaping. "Good evening, Miss Prentice." Momentarily, he could think of nothing to say, despite his Boston-bred good manners.

Goldie came to his rescue. She sat down on a sofa and said, "Please sit down. Hasn't it been a lovely day?" Then she drew him out about how he liked Yucca, the valley, and New Mexico. He soon felt at ease and the conversation flowed freely. She asked, "How's Thad these days?"

T. W. was surprised that she knew his uncle. "He's well, but far too busy. He would much rather be here in the valley than in Boston."

"We look forward to his visit each year. There are not many men of his caliber. So powerful and yet so human."

Uncle Thad at the Prentice Parlors? T. W. was just recovering from that shock when Jennifer came into the room. Such an opposite from Goldie. Everything about Jennifer was soft and subtle. Goldie was stunning, poised, in command. Jennifer was more like a fawn, but a fawn with blue eyes, black hair, fair skin, and a gentle smile.

"Good evening, you're very punctual," Jennifer said.

T. W. stood. "You look lovely, Jennifer."

"You're very gallant. Thank you."

Goldie said, "Have a good time."

The tall black man appeared and opened the door. As T. W. passed him, he said in a low voice, "Take good care of Miss Jennifer." It was not a threat but it was said in earnest, as a big brother would say it.

The dance was being held in the hotel's large restaurant. The tables had been removed so there would be plenty of space for dancing. As the young couple walked the two blocks, Jennifer was lighthearted and her laughter infectious. And T. W.'s slight apprehension disappeared.

Jennifer said, "This reminds me of my life back in St. Louis. We had lots of dances."

"You're a long way from St. Louis. Have you been in Yucca very long?"

"About six months. My mother died and I found out she had made some poor investments. Almost all the money was gone that my father had left her. Goldie came up to see how I was, and I just decided to come here with her."

"Do you like Yucca?"

"I think I could never leave the high country."

Laughing, T. W. said, "Wait. I know what you're going to say: The sky is such a pure blue and you can almost touch the clouds."

Jennifer smiled and took T. W.'s arm. "Haven't you come to feel the same way?"

"Not yet, but maybe I will."

"Anyway, you forgot one thing."

"What's that?"

"The people. They're so nice and friendly." She squeezed T. W.'s arm and he felt the softness of her breast.

The dance was in full swing when they arrived. The musicians had varying degrees of talent, but the general sound was good enough for dancing. Jennifer said, "I love that piece they're playing."

"Then let's dance, and not waste it."

T. W. had danced with many able partners, but not one could even come close to Jennifer's talent. There was never a push or a tug. She was truly as light as a feather. She anticipated every move. It seemed that her feet scarcely touched the floor, that he was just wafting her about. When the musicians stopped for a break, T. W. escorted her to one of the chairs lined up along the walls and he sat down beside her. Jennifer made the conversation move along easily as she talked about St. Louis, about morning horseback rides in the valley, about the beauty of the Sangre de Cristo mountains and the valley.

"Do you ride alone, Jennifer?"

"Sometimes, although George is usually along."

"George?" T. W. asked, surprised at the twinge of envy he felt.

"The man who works for us. You saw him tonight. He's also our butler, our bartender, and our guard."

"There are still Indians around, Jennifer. Now I will worry about you and your solo morning rides."

"You mustn't. George is usually with me and when he isn't, I don't go far."

T. W. saw Wash enter the ballroom. He said, "There's my teacher and good friend. Do you know Washington Carter?"

"Yes, he and George are friends. I've seen him often. I see two of Yucca's leading social figures have come in, Penelope Copeland and Britt MacKenzie. Do you know them?"

"I've met her in the Mercantile. I don't know him."

T. W. noted that although Penelope's hand was on the arm of MacKenzie, she was apart from him. She was obviously her own person, an independent spirit.

The musicians were still resting, so T. W. went to get punch for Jennifer. Britt and Penelope were already at the refreshment table and she introduced the two men. The three of them went to where Jennifer was sitting and the musicians went back to work. Britt asked Jennifer to dance. Alone with Penelope, T. W. could think of nothing to say.

She said, "Aren't you going to ask me to dance, Mr. Love?"

"Would you do me the honor?"

"I'd love to."

They danced for a few minutes without talking. Even the effortless dancing of Penelope could not compare with the wondrous skills of Jennifer. T. W. found himself wondering whether Penelope, if left penniless, could become an employee of Goldie Prentice. Probably not. If she couldn't find any other way to survive, she wouldn't work for Goldie, she would set up her own place.

"T. W., my stars, but you are hard to talk to."

"I'm sorry. I was just running a problem through my mind. I do apologize. Very rude of me."

"Apology accepted. I was just saying that I was quite surprised that you brought Miss Prentice to the dance."

"You mean you didn't know that I knew her? I met her this afternoon."

"No, I really didn't mean that."

"Are you questioning the propriety of my bringing her?"

"Well, yes. I guess I am."

"Wash Carter told me the people here respect Goldie and her employees."

"That's true, but respecting is, well . . . not the same as socializing with."

"You're saying that I should not have brought her?"

"It's really quite confusing, the more I think about it. Let's not talk about it anymore."

After several minutes, T. W. said, "I was quite surprised at seeing who is escorting you."

"What on earth could you mean by that?"

"It's confusing too. I can see how you would accept Britt MacKenzie at church. After all, churches are meant to help sinners, but I wonder about allowing him to bring you to the dance."

Penelope's dancing became stiffer. "I don't know what you mean."

"After talking to a number of people around town, I'm weighing the intention of their meaning when they say that MacKenzie swings a wide loop, or as one man put it, 'Britt's cows always seem to have twins.' "

"Why . . . why that means they think he's a cattle rustler. Why, that's terrible. Just terrible. Britt is very able and ambitious. Those men are just jealous."

"I hope you're right, Penelope. The fate of a cattle thief is not pleasant to think about."

"It sounds like you may believe those awful rumors."

"I'm not in a position to judge because I don't know him and I've only been here a few weeks."

"Well, take my word for it. Britt is going to be an important man in this Territory."

But T. W. could tell that Penelope was concerned. Her dancing was no longer effortless. When the musicians stopped, the men returned their partners and the couples separated.

Wash Carter came up and Jennifer said, "Hello, Wash. I haven't seen you dancing tonight."

"There doesn't seem to be a girl here with a dark enough complexion."

"Why don't you ask me? I'm sure T. W. won't mind."

"Wash knows it's all right with me."

"Thanks, Jennifer, but I just dropped over here to make sure T. W. has everything under control."

T. W. laughed. "No guns allowed in here, so I should be all right."

After a few more dances, Big John Oates came in and sidled slowly along the wall. T. W. noticed him giving some kind of a signal to MacKenzie and at the next intermission Britt took Penelope to a group of friends and left her. Big John had gone outside and Britt went out, too.

T. W. said, "Excuse me for a minute, Jennifer." He went over to Wash. "Did you see all that, Wash?"

"Yeah. I wonder what it's all about."

"Have you seen any of the Pothook crew in town?"

"I hadn't thought anything about it, but Big John's the only one I've seen and I didn't see him until a few minutes ago."

"Think we should leave for the JL?"

"If anything's been goin' on, we couldn't do anything about it till mornin' anyway. But I'll spread the word to

our men to take it easy tonight because we'll be huntin'
tracks as soon as it's light enough to see."

"Good. Did Magruder come to town?"

"No, but don't get any ideas. He never comes in on
Saturdays. I'll wait around and we can ride back together."

When the dance ended, T. W. walked Jennifer back to
the big white house. At the door she kissed him on the
cheek and said, "I don't know when I've had such a good
time. Thank you."

"My pleasure. A wonderful evening."

T. W. opened the door and watched Jennifer go up the
stairs. George was there and T. W. said, "I took good care
of her."

"Fine. Good night."

When they had left town, T. W. said, "How are you bet-
ting?"

"I'm bettin' we'll find a couple hundred head of JL stock
missin' from the east range."

"Wash, if the trail leads to the Pothook, Mr. MacKenzie
has bought himself some trouble."

"Maybe."

"Why maybe?"

"It'll be hard to find 'em. Pothook's as big as the JL.
They'll scatter 'em if they've got 'em."

"Can't we spot them by the brand?"

"Remember what I told you about the runnin' irons? A
good hand at that can easily make a JL look like a Pothook."

"And I suppose that if we have lost some, they can claim
it was Indians."

"Well, we'll know more in the mornin'."

CHAPTER 6

BEFORE FIRST LIGHT the JL crew was eating Chin's breakfast and wondering whether any cows would be missing. Magruder paired off the men and dispatched them to various parts of the JL to look for sign. If evidence were found of cows having been moved off the ranch, three spaced shots were to be fired and the others would converge on the area. Each man carried food for the noon meal. Wash and T. W. went due east. Like the others, they both strapped on revolvers and put rifles in their saddle scabbards. When they reached the eastern boundary of the JL, they worked north but saw nothing suspicious.

Wash said, "We should be seein' cows and calves around here. There were lots of 'em last week. There's good grass here and they wouldn't drift far away."

After they had turned and worked west, T. W. called out, "Wash, look over here."

Cattle had been gathered and then trailed off to the east. Wash dismounted, studied the ground, and said, "I think this happened yesterday afternoon."

"While we were all getting ready to go to town."

Wash fired the three spaced shots and then filled the empty chambers in the cylinder of the big Peacemaker. "Got a full clip in your Springfield?"

"Yes. Do we have to wait here?"

"No, they'll find us. They're pretty good trackers."

T. W.'s heart beat faster. They were not just hunting cattle. They were also hunting men. "Think it's Indians, Wash? I noticed that the horses didn't have shoes."

"I think so, but it could be whites tryin' to make us think

43

they're Indians. We've got to keep our eyes open. If they're white, they may be real good with rifles and six-guns. If they're Comanches, they might not even have rifles, but they're awful good with bows and arrows."

"I've read they're very accurate, even up to sixty yards."

"You read right. We're also gonna be outnumbered, no matter who they are. It would take more than two men to trail this many cows. Might be four or five, or even more since they were in a hurry."

The two JL men rode at a trot, following the trail left by the cattle and watching everywhere for signs of a possible ambush. Soon they were in the Sangre de Cristo foothills. Whoever the rustlers were, they knew exactly where they were headed. T. W. looked ahead and could see nothing but piñon-covered upslope with a background of towering, jagged precipitous walls of rock.

"Wash, are we heading for a pass?"

"Yeah. Poco Raton is straight ahead. You can't see it from here but those rustlers know where it is. I'm trying to figure out whether they're gonna bed down the cattle for the night or drive 'em through."

"Could they get through at night?"

"There should be a pretty good moon and if they know the pass real well, they could."

"How many head do you think they've got?"

"Two hundred, maybe two hundred and fifty. And they've moved 'em fast. They're experts. I think there might be six of 'em."

The trail started up and T. W. inhaled the fresh piñon fragrance. He thought of the Berkshires and his hunting trips with his uncle. Those expeditions were adventurous and lighthearted; this one was serious, dead serious. But T. W. had resolved to do everything he could to prevent death from becoming a part of this hunt.

Wash chose a level meadowlike area to stop for their noon meal. There was grass for the horses and they had water in their canteens. It felt good to get out of the saddle. They did not dare build a fire, so they ate jerky and cold sourdough biscuits, and lay on their backs for a few minutes. The horses needed rest, too.

"Wash, you know I don't hold with killing men on the spot for stealing cattle."

"Yes, I guess I do."

"I assume your plan of action is based on that principle."

"I don't have a plan yet. It'll depend on the situation. We'll have to work it out when we catch up with 'em. If we can do it your way, we will, but if we can't, we just can't."

"If we can surprise them, we can just hold them until Jim and the others get here. Then it will be pretty easy to take them in for a fair trail."

"Even if they're Indians?"

"That doesn't sound like you. I know you've fought and killed Indians, but you're not in the cavalry now. We have no moral or legal right to take a man's life."

"T. W., we'll do everything we can to make it come out your way, but remember, these owlhoots won't share your philosophy. The'll be shootin' to kill if they get a chance to shoot."

"That's it, Wash. We've got to get the drop on them."

"A couple of miles from here the trail divides. The trail they've got to take is the long way. We can pick up six or seven hours on 'em if we take the short one."

"Fine. By all means let's take the shorter one."

"Well, the short one isn't just short, it's also pretty rough. Actually it's dangerous."

"I'm ready when you think the horses are."

"All right, but I did warn you."

When they came to the fork in the trail, Wash swung to the right and they immediately started a sharp ascent. It was just a narrow path on the side of the mountain. T. W. admitted to himself that he was frightened when he looked to his right and straight down about two hundred feet. Sam seemed to be surefooted and if he were frightened, too, he didn't show it. After a couple of miles the trail widened out to about ten feet, but T. W. could see there had been a rock slide, with a steep sloping residue of shale. Wash stopped and looked at the impediment. T. W. rode up beside him.

"We stopped?"

"Depends."

"On what?"

"On how bad you want to catch the rustlers. If we have to go back now, they'll get all the way to the Pecos. And if they're selling to Comancheros, there'll be too many of 'em for us to do anything."

"If you think we can cross, I'm ready to try it."

"I think we can, but it will be kind of touch and go. Don't stop for anything. Keep movin'. And I think we better get down and lead the horses."

Wash started across. Some shale slid a little and went over the edge. It was a long time before the sound came back up. Wash reached solid rock and T. W. started across the twenty feet of treacherous shale. Sam followed without much urging. The horse seemed to be more confident than T. W. felt. Halfway across, however, some shale started to slide from under T. W.'s feet. He fought the urge to scramble, but the thin fragments continued to slip from under his boots. He felt himself losing his balance and beginning to go with the sliding rock. He dropped the reins and flung himself forward, but there was nothing solid beneath him and he fell. He twisted so he landed on his belly, hoping to flatten out and stop the shifting rock beneath him, but it didn't work and he felt himself sliding faster. He was helpless, but he tried to scramble and was still fighting as he went over the edge. He closed his eyes tight and waited for the long plunge to the rocks below.

He was slapped hard in the small of his back and then

on the back of his head. Bright flashes of light and then blackness.

Then there was a voice, from far away. The voice was calling his name. Vague, indistinct. His name, over and over. His head throbbed with pain, but he fought to open his eyes. Slowly he realized he was not on the ground or on a rock. His arms and legs were hanging down, unsupported. His back and shoulders were resting on small cylindrical somethings. He forced his eyes open and soon comprehended the amazing fact that he was in a tree, a great ponderosa whose smaller limbs had broken as he crashed through and whose larger limbs had finally stopped his fall. He looked up and there was Wash looking over the edge, calling to him.

When Wash saw that T. W. had opened his eyes, he called down to him, "Don't move! Your perch is pretty shaky. Do you think you have any broken bones?"

Very carefully T. W. tested each arm and leg. "No, I guess not, but I've got a terrible pain in my head."

He looked around and saw that he had fallen only about fifteen feet. He felt the back of his head with his hand and it came away with bright red, warm blood. "My head is cut."

"We'll have a look in a couple minutes. Now listen. I'm gonna throw you my rope. Snug the loop up under your arms. I'll tie the other end around my saddle horn and we'll ease you up. The only hard thing will be for you to get from the tree to the side of the canyon. We're over off the shale so there's a little angle for you to handle. Think you can do it?"

"Yes. When you're ready, let me know. I'll swing over with my legs out in front of me. It's only about ten feet, so I shouldn't hit too hard. Say, Wash, did Sam make it?"

"He's like a mountain goat. He's standin' over here like nothin's happened. Now, here comes the rope."

The rope caught on some branches, but T. W. got it and

snugged it under his arms. Wash tied the other end to the saddle horn and moved his horse to take up the slack. T. W. moved out on the branch as far as he dared.

"Ready, Wash?"

"Ready."

"Here I come!"

He hit hard and pain shot through his left ankle, but Wash started slowly hauling him up. When T. W. reached the ledge, Wash helped him onto solid ground.

"Thanks, friend."

"I thought you were a goner."

"So did I. I can't see too well. Things aren't in focus and I've never had a headache like this."

"Let me look. Well, it's not a deep gash. Just kind of a split and it's up where your hat won't bother it. I think the bleedin' has already just about stopped, but you might have a concussion. Better lie down for a while."

T. W. stretched out on his back. "Wash, how did Sam get across there?"

"He wasn't walkin' right behind you, and where he was the shale didn't move."

In about a half hour, T. W. said, "I'm ready." But his head pounded when Wash helped him into the saddle. His back was one huge area of pain and his ankle throbbed fiercely.

They moved slowly and soon were descending. By mid-afternoon they had rejoined the main trail. Wash dismounted to examine the tracks. He said, "We picked up a lot of time. They're maybe only an hour ahead. I'd say the cattle are really tired and movin' real slow, or we wouldn't have picked up so much on them."

"Wash, I've got to get out of this saddle for a few minutes. Every muscle in my body hurts."

Wash went to help him dismount, but T. W. said, "I've got to do this myself. Thanks just the same." He tried a few tentative walking steps and said, "They won't make it to the Pecos, will they?"

"I think they'll have to bed down. And they probably figure they had such a good head start that no one can catch 'em now."

"These cattle weren't taken to the Pothook. I don't see how MacKenzie could fit into this deal. Besides, he has too much to lose to get involved in this kind of thing."

"The only way I can figure it is that if he is the leader, he's runnin' a real big operation. A couple hundred head of cows taken from ten or twelve ranches and he'd have enough to send a big herd up the Goodnight-Loving trail to Denver or Cheyenne."

"Yes, if he had a herd of two thousand and sold them for forty dollars a head—the going price this summer— he'd gross eighty thousand dollars."

"That's big money, even after he pays off his expensive help."

"Of course we are assuming it is MacKenzie and that he is sending up those trail herds. But if he's doing what we think he's doing, and if he's also making money from legitimate ranch operations, he is, or he soon will be, a very rich man."

"And I don't think he wants to be just rich. I think he's plannin' on bein' territorial governor or somethin' else big in politics."

"You know, Wash, Penelope Copeland would be the perfect wife for a governor, wouldn't she? She's lovely, well mannered, and educated."

"Sure is."

"Well, I know we should be on our way." T. W. walked with obvious pain and caught up Sam's reins and struggled into the saddle.

"We'd better walk the horses. You don't look so good, and we'd better be careful. The rustlers might drop off a rear lookout."

It embarrassed him, but T. W. held on to the saddle horn. It eased the pain somewhat, but the agony grew and he was nearly driven to tell Wash he couldn't stand it anymore. He was determined, though. He would not ask for any special treatment. This was not a game: men might die before this day was ended.

Wash pulled up his buckskin. "We better stop and eat the rest of our jerky and biscuits. We don't know what's gonna happen up ahead."

T. W. hesitated and Wash could read what was on T. W.'s mind. He said, "You took an awful wallop this afternoon. If you need help gettin' back in the saddle, I'll help you. I don't see how you can ride at all."

T. W. lay on his side and ate the cold food. After fifteen minutes, Wash said, "About three or four miles from here there's a small box canyon that would be just right for holdin' a small herd overnight. We can go up here through the piñon and work around to take a look. They'll have guards at the entrance if that's where they decide to bed down."

Wash helped T. W. back into the saddle and they picked their way up the side of the mountain. Every step Sam took jarred T. W.'s aching head and jolted his protesting back muscles, but he clamped his teeth together and tried to maintain an expressionless face.

Wash stopped again. "It's only a few hundred yards to the canyon rim. We better leave the horses here. We don't want a whinny to give us away."

At the rim, they went down on their bellies and squirmed to the edge. It was not quite dark and they could see plainly. Wash's logic had been sound. The longhorns were grazing on lush grass in the small canyon. A creek ran through the middle, carrying the last of the year's snowmelt from the peaks far above.

"That's beautiful, Wash. You know, this would be a great

place to build a cabin to come to when a man needs to get away from everybody and everything."

"Yes, I often think of this place. It's so far up here that it belongs to nobody."

"Wash, I don't see any Indians or cowhands with the cattle."

"That's the first problem we've gotta solve. Are they all down at the entrance, or are they posted around up here? We might walk right into somebody with orders to shoot on sight."

CHAPTER 7

"WASH, YOU'RE NOT forgetting about taking these men in for trial, are you?"

"No, but I'll tell you, I don't intend for either you or me to die for that principle. So, if your Peacemaker is down tight in the holster, you better loosen it and keep yourself alert. These rannies, whoever they are, will shoot at you if they see you first. Just don't you forget that."

The eastern sky was dark and the only vestige of day was a small cloud that caught the last rays of the sun and held them briefly in a golden-red hue. Then suddenly the color was gone and the darkness descended. The moon was nearly at its zenith and provided some illumination.

Wash said, "Well, we can see, but they can see too."

"Wash, what would your plan be if Shorty or Brick were here instead of me?"

"We'd find a spot to pick off as many of them as we could in a surprise attack. We'd probably get three or four of 'em if we worked it right and the rest of 'em would take off. Then in the mornin' we'd start back with the cattle when the rest of the crew got here."

"Well, what's your plan now, since I'm the one here with you?"

"That's a problem. I've tried to figure a way we could surround 'em, but I don't see how that's possible with only two of us."

"When do you estimate that Magruder and the rest of them will get here?"

"They don't know about the shortcut, so I wouldn't expect them till tomorrow, late mornin', probably."

"I guess we should try to find out where the rustlers are."

"Yep. You wait here. I'll go have a look."

Wash moved away and T. W. marveled at how quietly such a big man could move across the ground.

T. W. kept alert, with his rifle on his lap and his finger on the trigger guard. The pain in his head was less intense, but he needed support for his back, so he found a large rock to lean on where he could see down the slope. Time passed and T. W. began to worry. After what seemed to be too long for Wash's reconnaissance, T. W. saw a shadowy movement downslope. He slowly moved his Winchester to a position for shooting and watched intently. Another shadow seemed to move. He put the rifle to his shoulder, sighted down the barrel, and put his finger on the trigger. Wash had said to shoot first, but was the movement his imagination? Was he being spooked? He must not shoot unless absolutely necessary. It would put the rustlers on their guard and destroy the surprise element.

A hoarse whisper said, "Don't shoot. It's me, Wash."

"Come on up," T. W. said, but he did not lower the rifle.

"Glad you're awake."

"What did you find out?"

"There are six of 'em. They look like Indians, but they don't act like Indians. Four are asleep and two are posted up in the rocks near the entrance, where it's hard to see 'em. If they're really Comanches, I think they would all be asleep. And their horses don't look like Indian horses. They're too big, and they all have saddles."

T. W. was quiet, thinking. Then he said, "So the only way we can capture them is to get the guards first. Is that possible?"

"I don't see how. Even if we could get to them without makin' any noise, how could we capture 'em without makin' noise?"

"What happens if we wait until morning when they're busy getting the cows out of the canyon?"

"We can't take 'em without some shootin'. Somebody would get killed. Maybe us. Remember, it's six against two."

"Is there a way down to the canyon floor from here?"

"Not on horses. There's one place we could get down with the horses but it's way down at the other end. And remember what I told you about bein' afoot around long-horns. You stand a good chance of havin' one of those horns go in your belly and come out your back."

"Then what you're actually saying is that there is no way to get back the JL steers and capture the rustlers without violence, without somebody getting killed."

"That's the way I see it. And if we wait for Magruder and the boys, that herd will be at the Pecos and we won't have enough guns to take back what belongs to us."

"Our only course of action, then, is to shoot two of them so we can apprehend four of them, and we can't try that until morning?"

"I can't see any other way."

"There must be an alternative. Or at least a plan that will lessen the chance of bloodshed."

After some thought, T. W. continued, "What if we wait until morning, then strike just as the guards come down out of their vantage points. We should have them all together for a short period of time."

"While they eat, maybe. I'm willin', but we'll have to separate. One on each side of the canyon mouth. And we've got to have spots where we'll be protected, because I don't think they're just gonna surrender without some kind of fight."

T. W. and Wash took turns sleeping. When the first faint hint of gray appeared in the east, Wash went to his horse and started to make his way around the far end of the canyon. He would do his coyote bark when he was in position at the canyon mouth and ready for action. T. W. carefully worked his way over the rocky terrain. It was just light enough so he could pick solid rock to step on and not start any stones rolling to alert the guard on his side. He went as close as he dared and waited behind an outcropping until the guard left to join the others. Wash should be on station, so T. W. worked in to where the guard had been.

The fierce pounding in his head was nearly gone, but it seemed to have worked its way to his heart. It had never pulsed at this rate except during strenuous exercise, and he had certainly been in tight situations before. Plenty of them. He had not been this tense in the China Sea when a typhoon had tossed the old square-rigged, three-masted White Cloud around like a toy. Unflinchingly, he had gone up in the rigging to take in sail that day. In the Maine lumber camp, he had stood face-to-face with a crazed lumberjack who had already killed one man with his razor-sharp two-edged axe, and T. W. had talked the poor man into surrendering when others were ready to shoot him.

T. W. tried to take stock of his emotions and decided his tension was derived from two fears. First, he did not want Wash to be injured for what T. W. thought was right. Second, he feared that perhaps he was doing the wrong thing. Maybe his Eastern moralities really were out of place in untamed New Mexico, but he had talked a lot about justice and law, that every man deserved a fair trial—now he was being put to the test.

It was light enough to see the rustlers clearly. They were wrapped in blankets to ward off the early-morning mountain chill. They had streaks of paint on their faces and moccasins on their feet. Two wore beaded headbands. But they all needed shaves and none had the skin coloring of an Indian. One of them had built a small, smokeless fire, and all six were gathered around drinking coffee. This was the moment to act.

The coyote barked. T. W. stood up and leveled his Winchester at the group. Wash shouted, "You're surrounded. Throw up your hands!"

The rustlers dropped their cups and slowly stood up and raised their arms. One of them started to move for his pistol and T. W. placed a shot at his feet. The man stopped and they all looked around to locate those who had sprung the trap on them. There was some low-voiced conversation that T. W. could not make out. They were probably talking about the odds for making a break.

Wash called out, "The first one who moves will die. Don't try it. You've all got six-guns under those blankets. Don't try for 'em. You with the blue blanket, drop the blanket. Now very slowly unbuckle your gunbelt and throw it this way. No sudden move or you're dead."

The other five followed the same procedure. None of them threw the gunbelts very far, but that was to be expected.

Wash shouted to T. W., "The rest of you go and get your horses and ride down to meet our friends. I'll cover these owlhoots while you're gone. I'm usin' my Winchester '73 so they know how many cartridges I've got in the magazine."

T. W. moved as fast as he could and just as he reached Sam, he heard one shot. It had to be Wash. One of the rustlers must have tried him. When T. W. rode up to the canyon mouth, one of the men was sitting on the ground holding his lower leg. The others were still standing with their arms raised, though not as high as before.

Wash said, "Collect their gunbelts, T. W., but don't get between me and them any more than you can help."

T. W. collected the belts and piled them near Sam. He turned to face the rustlers, holding his Winchester at his hip with the safety off, then said, "All right, Wash, you can get your horse now."

After Wash left, the rustlers looked at each other. The

truth was finally dawning on them. There were only two men "surrounding" them.

A tall, lanky rustler fixed his slate blue eyes on T. W. and said, "I think we can take this one. I never saw a four-eyed bastard that could shoot straight. And I think this one's yellow anyway. I think he's shakin' in his boots."

A short, dark rustler standing next to the tall one said, "I'm not sure you're right, Slim. He holds that rifle like he knows how to shoot it."

"If you're wondering which one I'll shoot first, Slim, it'll be you. This is a '73 I'm holding and I've got fourteen shots left in the magazine."

Wash was going to be gone at least fifteen minutes and T. W. was worried whether he could shoot to kill if any of them did move on him. The skinny one sensed his indecision and was doing his best to stir up the others. T. W. stopped talking. He knew it was part of Slim's plan to destroy his concentration and he was not going to let it happen. Slim started to talk again and T. W. said one more thing. "You *will* be first, Slim."

"I don't think you'll shoot anybody, sonny." To the others he said, "When I give the word, everybody scatter real quick and rush him." The other four still on their feet nodded and Slim said, "Ready, boys."

T. W. sighted his rifle at Slim's belly.

Slim said, "He's yellow. He knows it and we know it. On your toes."

T. W. raised his rifle, aimed at Slim's right shoulder, and squeezed the trigger. The .44-40 slug spun Slim around and he dropped to the ground. T. W. moved his sight to the next man in line, who looked down at Slim and said, "I guess you're wrong, Slim." Then he looked up at T. W. and said, "I'm not movin'. Don't shoot."

Nobody else talked or moved, but T. W. kept the rifle at his shoulder for several minutes until he was certain the

threat had passed. In about ten minutes Wash came galloping up and T. W. gave him the story.

Wash said, "Keep your rifle on 'em. I'm gonna tie up the
ones still standin'." He went to the outlaws and returned
with their ropes. He motioned the first one out of the line
and made him lie down on his belly. He tied his hands
behind his back and tied his feet. He did the same with
the others. Slim sat up and Wash said, "I guess you don't
have any plans for goin' anywhere. Any movin' around
and you're gonna lose a lot more blood." Slim did not
answer.

When Magruder and the crew arrived later in the morning there was some good-natured joking about what had
taken them so long, but the occasion was too serious to
prolong it. The rustlers were looked at closely and Shorty
remembered seeing two of them in Yucca several weeks
before. "They're all hired gunslicks," he said. "The one
with the bad leg gunned down a Rockin' W hand for no
reason at all."

Brick said, "What're we standin' around for? Let's find
a cottonwood and get it over with. Any trees back in the
box canyon?"

It was testing time again for T. W. Love. He had known
it would come.

CHAPTER 8

"WAIT A MINUTE, boys. These men have not been tried."

Jim Magruder looked at T. W. and said, "We caught them with the herd. They're our cows and we trailed them all the way. Is there any question they're guilty?"

"I don't think there is, Jim. And I think the judge will find them guilty. But that's the responsibility of the court."

"If we know the judge will convict 'em," Brick asked, "why go to all the trouble?"

"It's also the court's duty to determine what the sentence should be. We don't have that power."

Magruder said, "That's probably the way it should be done, but do you know where the nearest judge is, T. W.?"

"Yes, in Santa Fe, and I know it's a long way to take six men who have been stealing cattle. But we simply do not have the authority to convict and hang them."

Jim Magruder said patiently, "We're living in a part of the country where horse thieves and rustlers are given their justice at the place they're caught. It's the way it's done. It's accepted by everyone."

"Jim, it's not the way it should be done, though. If there is ever going to be law and order in the Territory it must begin with the good, honest citizens. Citizens who obey the law. Also, Jim, we need to let the people of this territory know that these men were trying to throw the blame on Indians. If they had escaped, everyone would have said the rustlers were Comanches and that could have stirred up Indian trouble again."

Magruder thought for a moment. "We certainly don't

need any more Comanche problems, but as far as that's concerned we can just tell folks they were fake Indians."

"But if there is a trial, it will be published in *The New Mexican* and it'll be read all over the territory. Everybody will know."

Brick said, "T. W. makes sense, but I still don't know if it's worth all the trouble."

Shorty said, "It's sure enough a long way to go with these varmints."

Wash Carter said, "Look, we all know it's a long way and a lot of trouble, but T. W. and I have already gone to a lot of trouble, and we took a big risk to capture these men instead of shootin' 'em. Anyway, I think he's right and I think we've got lots to do besides standin' around jawin' about the situation."

Wash turned to Magruder for orders. The ramrod said, "All right, boys, they're probably right. Wash, you go with T. W. to Santa Fe. And Shorty, you go along too. The rest of you, let's get started with these cows."

Wash and Shorty improvised bandages for the wounded rustlers and the JL men started moving the cattle out of the canyon. T. W. said to Magruder, "Jim, there's another good reason for taking them to Santa Fe."

"What's that?"

"The court might find out who is running this operation. We've only apprehended some of the little men. This won't stop until the big man is caught."

"You're right, but these men won't talk. They'd be killed."

"Jim, you have any idea who he might be?"

"No. I've sure thought about it a lot, but I can't come up with anybody. I think whoever runs it must do it from some distance away."

"I'm sure you have considered Britt MacKenzie. I understand his herd has increased at a phenomenal rate."

"He just doesn't seem to fit."

"Have you ever seen any steers on his range that looked like he altered the brand to make it a JL?"

"I'll tell you, he's got a big crew working his spread and none of us have gotten close enough to get a good look before some of his bunch run us off."

"Doesn't that make you wonder about him a little?"

"Yes, but nothing else about him seems to fit a Comanchero boss. Some ranchers are real private about their range. And they got a right to be if they want to."

T. W. rode to catch up with Wash and Shorty and the prisoners. Was there a special reason Magruder wanted to hang the rustlers right away? To make sure they couldn't talk? Could it possibly be MacKenzie and Magruder? If they were in it together, where did Jim keep all his money? Jim was a likable man; he worked hard and he was able. Although he seemed to be honest and loyal, an investigator could leave no stone unturned.

On the trek to Santa Fe, the rustlers had to ride with their feet tied by a rope under the horse and their hands tied to the saddle horn. It was dangerous if something frightened a horse, but it seemed a secure way to travel. At night the men were tied and the JL men took turns standing watch.

In Santa Fe, the Fifth District judge took the case right away. The prosecutor and the judge tried to get information about who was organizing the Comanchero operation and carrying out the plans, but the six men would not talk. They were convicted and sentenced to five years in prison. The judge praised T. W. and Wash for capturing and bringing in the rustlers. He said, "If New Mexico is ever to become a state, we must rid ourselves of the abominable lynch law, hanging men without a legal trial. All citizens must come to think as you do."

T. W. asked if the U. S. marshal was trying to stop the highly profitable business of the Comancheros. The judge said the marshal was doing all he could with a staff that was much too small. "We just don't have enough deputies to police such a large area."

That night, in their room at the big La Fonda hotel on the old plaza, T. W. asked Wash whether the prison in Santa Fe was a good one.

"It's not like ones back East. I don't think those yahoos could bust out, but I think they could be busted out if someone wanted to do it."

Before leaving for Yucca the next morning, T. W. went to see the marshal, an affable, older man who readily agreed to cooperate when T. W. outlined his plan. The marshal would contact the banks in northern New Mexico and obtain the names of all depositors who had large accounts. Then he would supply those names to T. W.

"But you can't send this information to me at the JL."

"Will you come to Santa Fe to get it?"

T. W. thought of Jennifer Prentice and somehow he felt he could trust her. The marshal wrote down the name and then with a knowing glance asked, "Any relation to Goldie?"

"Her sister. I guess everybody in northern New Mexico knows Goldie or knows about her. Thanks for your cooperation, Marshal."

The JL men went to the livery for their horses and were soon riding south on the well-traveled Camino Real. Shorty looked back toward the city and said, "I'll be back this fall, girls."

T. W. asked, "You come up here very often, Shorty?"

"Once a year, after the fall roundup. I come and stay a week unless my money runs out first."

"What's the big attraction?"

"Those young Spanish women with their dark eyes and their black hair. And those women dancin' that flamenco dance just do stir up a man's blood."

"I'd like to see that dance. I've read about how fast and exciting it is."

Wash said, "It's more than fast and exciting. Shorty's right about it givin' a man ideas."

When the trio reached Yucca, T. W. said, "Let's go in the Palace and wash some of the dust out of our throats."

Shorty and Wash ordered whiskey and T. W. ordered his usual sarsaparilla. It wasn't dark yet and the evening crowd had not arrived. Shorty was studying the painting of the big blonde behind the bar. T. W. thought that Goldie could probably increase her business if she had copies placed in all the saloons, and maybe in every ranch bunkhouse.

T. W. said he had an errand to do. He put a silver dollar on the bar and said, "Heinie, give my two good friends whatever they want. We've had a hard couple of days." Then he walked the two blocks to Prentice Parlors, opened the picket gate, admired the petunias along the walk, rang the bell, and waited. George opened the door, invited T. W. to enter, and said, "It's kind of early but I'll check to see who's available."

"Oh, I'm not here for . . . uh, that. I just want to talk to Miss Jennifer for a few minutes. If she can see me."

In a few minutes Jennifer appeared in the doorway and T. W. stood. "Hello, Jennifer."

"Good afternoon, T. W. Please sit down."

She sat down next to him, immaculately groomed, and wearing a becoming blue gingham gown that merely hinted at the attractively slender body inside it. "George said you wanted to talk to me, T. W."

"For just a moment, if you're not too busy."

T. W. was surprised at his feelings about Jennifer. He felt the same as he did when he was making a social call on any "proper" Boston girl of his acquaintance. It all seemed the same, well almost the same.

Without explaining about the contents, he told her the U. S. marshal in Santa Fe was going to send him a letter. It was confidential and he could not have it sent to the JL.

"Although we really don't know each other very well, I have the feeling that I can trust you and I have asked the marshal to send it in your care. If you don't want to have it sent here, I'll wire him not to do it."

"That's not a problem. I'm flattered that you trust me, but I'm also worried."

"Worried?"

"Yes. There are powerful and ruthless men here, T. W., and if you get in their way, they wouldn't hesitate to kill you. I don't know what they are doing, but I do know there is a great deal of money and power involved." She looked squarely into his eyes and said, "You are too young, and too nice, to die."

"Well, thank you, Jennifer. And thank you for helping me. I really appreciate it. I do know there is danger and I'll be careful."

George opened the door for T. W. when he was leaving and stepped out on the porch. "Mr. Love," he said, "don't get Miss Jennifer involved in anything that might get her hurt."

Before T. W. could reply, George had gone back inside the house.

CHAPTER 9

RIDING BACK TO the ranch, T. W. was disturbed and confused. Jennifer Prentice was the problem. She had culture. She was sensitive. She was educated. And she was beautiful and shapely. She was everything a man could want for a wife. Except for that one great drawback. How could he be so interested in a woman who made her living in the upper parlors at Prentice Parlors? He could not let himself think about her doing the things she must do night after night.

What would his uncle say? T. W. could hardly imagine. Yet, Goldie had spoken of him as if she knew him. T. W. tried to put things in their proper perspective. Probably his uncle would say something like "Keep each thing in its proper place. If you find yourself in need of the lady's companionship from time to time, that's all right, but keep it the way it ought to be."

Well, Thad Love had been married to a Boston lady who had died tragically young. He had never remarried. He still was not old, fifty years at the most, though T. W. had never asked him about his age. Thad had raised him, giving him the same advantages as the son of any prominent Boston investment banker, which included sending his nephew to expensive schools.

T. W. had never known his parents. His father was the younger brother of Thad and had served with Colonel Stephen Kearny in the war with Mexico. He had loved the Santa Fe area so much that he had returned to Boston, married his childhood sweetheart, and taken her out to the high Estancia Valley. They were establishing the John

Love cattle ranch when raiding Comanches had killed them, burned the buildings, and kidnapped T. W., who was one year old. Thad had come out from Boston and ransomed T. W. He had also paid off the debts on the young couple's ranch, bought the ranch, and put the purchase money in a trust fund for little Terrence. T. W. knew of the trust fund, but Thad would never let him use any of it. He said, "It will keep until you graduate from Harvard."

Now here he was, Terrence Waddington Love, returned to the land of his birth, and possibly falling in love with Jennifer Prentice, a star of the upper parlors. What would the reactions of his parents have been? It was all too confusing and T. W. was glad when they rode into JL headquarters. Realistically, Jennifer probably entertained no romantic notions about a Boston dude who had to wear glasses, so all the speculation was for nothing anyway.

Jim Magruder came out to greet them. "Just in time for chow. Might know you all would show up in time for that."

Shorty said, "No problem about that. Nobody in town cooks as good as Chin."

By the time the three men had cared for their horses, Chin had the meal on the long bunkhouse table. The conversation turned quickly to what had happened in Santa Fe. The men thought that what happened was probably all right, but there was also agreement when Brick said, "A five-year sentence ain't much, especially when you figure a year off for good behavior."

That night, as usual, T. W. went into Thad's big room and looked at the collection of books on the shelves. He chose a volume of Ralph Waldo Emerson's essays and poetry and turned to an essay with which he was familiar, the one on Character. He found this passage:

Character denotes habitual self-possession, habitual regard to interior and constitutional motives, a balance not to be overset or easily disturbed by outward events and opinion, and by implication points to the source of right motive. . . . There is no end to the sufficience of character . . . it can do without what is called success; it cannot but succeed.

The reading bolstered his resolve. He would proceed on the course he believed was the right one. Then he turned to an Emerson poem called "Give All to Love." He read the first stanza:

> *Give all to love;*
> *Obey thy heart;*
> *Friends, kindred, days,*
> *Estate, good fame,*
> *Plans, credit and the Muse,—*
> *Nothing refuse.*

He placed the book back on the shelf and got ready for bed. When he lay down he considered how good it was to be home and in his own bed. As he drifted off to sleep he found it interesting that he had been in the valley for only a few weeks and already was thinking of it as home.

The next morning, Magruder sent Wash and T. W. to Yucca for supplies, including feed for Chin's flock of chickens. The JL was one of the few ranches in the valley that had fresh eggs. Although they joshed Chin about his flock, the men in the crew appreciated the eggs for breakfast, and Chin knew it. He only feigned anger when they kidded him about his "feathered herd."

Wash and T. W. went to the Mercantile for the chicken feed and grocery staples Chin needed. Penelope Copeland saw them and left the dry-goods-and-clothing area to speak to them.

"Good morning, gentlemen," she said cheerfully. "I wanted to tell you both how much I admire your taking those rustlers in for trial instead of taking the law into your own hands. There are not many men in the valley who would have placed themselves in such danger for that cause."

Wash said, "It was T. W.'s idea. The rest of us would have given them justice at the end of a rope."

"Well, you should not have had to risk your lives," she said. "We should have a sheriff for the town and a marshal for the valley. Britt has been trying to convince people of that, but not many are willing to pay what it would cost us."

T. W. said, "The time will come. For now we must do what we can as private citizens. By the way, did Britt lose any stock?"

"Not that I know of, but others did. Apparently it was a large operation, but the ones you caught were the only ones that didn't succeed."

"Maybe," T. W. said, "they are afraid to try it with Pothook cattle because Britt has so many men who are expert with guns."

After some small chatter about how much the valley needed rain, Penelope went back to arrange a display of new bolts of cloth. T. W. watched her. He was impressed by her principles, as much as her good looks. He said, "There is a woman of rare beauty, and strong character. Wash, she'd make a fine wife for some man."

"It will take a lot of man to get a yes to his proposal."

"Is MacKenzie man enough?"

"Well, he's rich and powerful enough, but there s something about him. He's weak somewhere."

"You know, Wash, maybe his ambitious posturing is just an attempt to cover up that weak spot."

T. W. and Wash were loading their wagon when George of Prentice Parlors came to the Mercantile. He said hello but did not stop to talk. Wash said, "Now there's a man, T. W. If he was white, he'd be a leader in this territory. He was one of the few black officers in Sherman's army. I didn't know him, but I heard about him."

"Why is he working for Goldie?"

"She pays him. He doesn't like ranch work, so he doesn't have much choice. The job's not bad. When one of Goldie's customers gets a little rowdy, George doesn't have to throw him out, he just looks at him. I know he saves his pay, and he has some sort of a plan. He reads law books that he borrows from the only lawyer in town."

"I have the feeling that I would like to have George on our side if there's ever any trouble."

That afternoon Magruder sent T. W. and Wash to the north range to move cattle west to where the grass was better and they would be safer from rustlers who might try to drive them east to the Pecos. By late afternoon the two had rounded up about a hundred head and were looking for more before starting west.

T. W. said, "Looks like a thunderstorm building up over the Jemez range."

"I think we're gonna get wet. Good thing you brought your fish."

"My fish?"

"Your oilskin slicker."

"Oh, yes. You know, this will be the first time it's rained since I've been here."

"In about a half hour, we're gonna wish we were back at headquarters. Be sure your rifle and pistol are under your fish."

The clouds began to look ugly and grew in size and darkness. Lightning flashed and the cattle became skittish, their eyes showing their fear. Wash and T. W. had trouble keeping the herd moving. One large blue roan steer in particular kept breaking out of the herd. T. W. decided to do what Wash had taught him to do when a breakaway became troublesome—rope him and throw him hard to the ground. That usually took the cantankerousness out of him. T. W. went after him, swinging his loop as Sam raced over the uneven ground. He cast his loop over the wide-spread horns and tightened it around the neck. Sam skidded to a stop and braced himself. The big blue hit the end of the rope and was slammed hard to the ground, but the sudden strain broke the latigo tied to the center-fire cinch. T. W., still riding the saddle, went flying through the air over Sam's head and landed hard.

T. W. and the steer slowly got to their feet at the same time. T. W. looked for Sam, who had not gone far, but this kind of thing had never happened to the horse before and he was confused. The steer was already pawing dirt and T. W. knew he could not get to Sam. He reached for his Peacemaker, but he had lost it in the fall. He could not even see where it had landed. The roan was about to charge. There was no tree to hide behind, not even a juniper close by. All T. W. could do was stand his ground and try to leap aside at the last moment.

Big blue stopped pawing and began moving. Slowly at first, then gathering headway. T. W. was poised on the balls of his feet, wishing he was wearing rugby shoes for better footing. The steer came fast now and T. W. waited. As the long, pointed horns and sharp hooves thundered down on him, T. W. dived to the right. The steer hooked with his horn as he passed and caught T. W.'s right foot, but the boot leather was good and the tip of the horn did not penetrate. The next pass was going to be touch and go. The ankle hurt and might not be of much use. Sam was watching the strange episode and T. W. knew if he could just get on the horse, the steer would stop his attack because cattle didn't attack men on horses. But Sam was too far away.

The steer turned quickly, snorted, and began to move again. T. W. saw Wash coming fast, already whirling his reata. Wash cast the loop up under the steer's hind legs. His horse skidded to a stop and the steer went down heavily fifteen feet in front of T. W.

Wash shook his loop free, the steer got to his feet, and Wash choused him back to the rest of the bunch. The old blue roan seemed glad to go.

T. W. looked up at Wash. "You saved my life."

"Oh, I don't know. You probably could have dodged him all day." Wash laughed and added, "He's pretty old. He should have gone up the trail several years ago. Must be good at hidin' when we're roundin' them up."

"Wash, what's so funny?"

"Why, I've heard of a latigo breakin' and puttin' a man in a situation like that, but I'd never seen it. It's kind of funny."

"Unless it happens to you."

"Are you hurt?"

"He hooked my ankle hard, but it didn't puncture my boot. I guess my pride is hurt, too."

"I've got some leather and an awl I carry around for emergencies. Let's mend your latigo before that big cloud opens up on us."

By the time Wash had laced the latigo back together, T. W. could see how he must have looked—afoot and trying to dodge the steer. "I guess it could look funny to someone watching."

"At least as long as nobody got hurt."

When the first big raindrops hit, T. W. had found his Colt and was mounted again. Wash showed him how to put the oilskin over the pommel and back over the cantle. The two men moved the cattle along and the rain came hard, driven almost horizontal by the strong northwest gale. The cattle would not walk into the face of the storm and the men finally had to let them alone when they turned their rumps to the lashing rain and drifted slowly with the storm. The water poured down off the brim of T. W.'s big hat and he was glad it had such a wide brim and solid crown.

When the rain stopped, the air was fresh and clean.

T. W. inhaled deeply and admired the newly washed picture he saw. Even the longhorns were clean. Sudden rain on the high plains was a new experience. Rain at sea washed things clean, but it didn't have the fragrance of the freshened vegetation to bring the added pleasure.

Wash and T. W. rolled their slickers and tied them back of their cantles. Soon they had the cattle turned and headed in the right direction. They approached a narrow arroyo and Wash went ahead to check out the situation. He came back and said, "Let's hurry them across. There may be a flash flood comin' down from higher ground."

Hollering and swinging their lariats, the men chased the cattle across. Suddenly Wash said, "Listen."

T. W. heard a roar and Wash told him to go back near the arroyo. "You've never seen a flash flood before. You can catch up easy."

It was an amazing sight. A wall of water was raging down the arroyo. It was three feet high, foaming brown and carrying a large log and some smaller brush and debris. Anyone caught in it could be drowned if his head hit a log or a big boulder.

After they left the cattle safely in a west pasture the men returned to the JL. That night T. W. went into Thad Love's study to write to his uncle. It was time to report on his first three weeks. He wrote: "Life is real, life is earnest." Was that Wordsworth's line . . . or Longfellow's? And the day had been ample proof of how right the poet was. Nevertheless, T. W. would have to admit he had no solid clue about why the JL was losing money. But he did have a lot to tell, about many things, and he did have some suspicions.

CHAPTER 10

HE STARTED WITH the suspicions. Britt MacKenzie was at the top of the list, but T. W. had to admit he had nothing definite on him. It was mostly circumstantial, even after the cattle-rustling episode and taking the rustlers to Santa Fe for trial. He could report for certain that the losses seemed to be caused by rustling, but he did not know who was behind it. Jim Magruder seemed to be honest, but he was still a suspect. The JL crew was a hardworking bunch and seemed to be honest and loyal. Wash Carter had become a true friend. He was impressed by Penelope Copeland's beauty and education.

T. W. went on to tell what he had learned about life as a working cowhand and how much he was enjoying all of it. He concluded:

> *This country and this life make one feel like he is a whole man. There is frequent conflict of some kind. Sometimes fighting nature, sometimes fighting other men, and sometimes fighting himself. I think the most difficult foe is a man's inner self. But each victory makes the next fight a little easier to win.*

T. W. leaned back in the big chair and thought about what he had written. He could see why his uncle was tempted to leave Boston and live here. But maybe moving West was a romantic notion, an idle dream. Could a man like Thad Love be content living in the valley? Or were the ranch and the high country just a refuge he turned to when business was too pressing, when life was too much for him?

T. W. realized he too might be fantasizing about the West because he was not really ready for Beacon Hill society life, for marriage and being in an office all day. After the last few weeks he shuddered at the thought of being confined to an office.

The next morning T. W. told Magruder he wanted to ride the boundary between the JL and the Pothook to see if there had been any activity along there. Magruder said he would ride along. Midmorning they saw where about twenty longhorns had been driven from JL range to Pothook territory. There had been only one rider, riding an unshod horse.

"What do you make of it, Jim?"

"Well, some Pothook stock could have drifted over here and someone herded them back."

"You really think that?"

"Seems more likely that someone on Pothook has hazed some JL stock."

"Let's follow this trail and find out. We have a right to investigate, don't we?"

"We surely do. Let's go."

The trail was easy to follow, and soon the two men came to a spot where there had been a fire and a lot of activity.

"Branding, Jim?"

"Sure looks like it. Let's go on."

Several miles farther, the trail merged with the tracks of other cattle. The small herd had been moved in with a larger bunch already grazing there.

T. W. said, "I see some steers over east. Let's take a look."

No sooner had Magruder said, "I'm kinda worried about going this far on Pothook land," than a rider came galloping straight for them out of an arroyo.

With no preliminaries, the man shouted, "Who are you?"

"I'm Jim Magruder and this is T. W. Love. I'm foreman of the JL. Who are you?"

"It don't matter who I am. Get off Pothook range!"

"We're neighbors and we're lookin' for strays that headed this way. Seen any steers wearin' the JL brand?"

"No, now git! My orders are to keep everybody off Pothook land."

T. W. did not like what he saw. The man wore two guns, low on his thighs, with the holsters tied down.

Magruder said, "You must be new. We're friends of Britt's. The two ranches have always helped each other about strays. Sometimes we even run our roundups together."

"I didn't ride over here to talk. This ain't your land, now git off it."

Magruder started to speak. "If you'll just ask Britt about—"

The Pothook man's right hand suddenly held his pistol, pointed at Magruder's belly. "I ain't sayin' it agin. Git!"

Magruder and T. W. exchanged glances, turned their horses, and headed for the JL. Magruder said, "I wish Britt wouldn't hire that kind of rider."

"He must have a reason. No one hires gunmen just to punch cows, does he, Jim? There's something he doesn't want us to see."

They rode in silence for several miles, then T. W. asked, "Would you be able to tell if a JL brand had been changed to a Pothook?"

"The J and the L are close and could be run together. Then the iron could be run across the top, and the bottom of the L could be run up a little and over to the left. As soon as the scab came off, you probably couldn't tell, especially after the hair grew out a little."

"How about the earmark?"

"That could be changed real easy to look like MacKenzie's."

"So the only way we could prove anything would be to catch them in the act or when the scab is still there."

T. W. looked back. The man was still sitting his horse, watching to make sure they continued on their way. "Jim, what do you think would have happened if we had insisted on checking out those cattle?"

"I just don't know. I don't want anybody killed and he looked like he would use those two guns."

T. W. thought he might be unreasonably suspicious, but he questioned whether Magruder should have been more insistent about checking out those steers. After all, twenty steers would bring between four hundred and five hundred dollars at the railroad. If MacKenzie was the ringleader of the rustlers, Pothook had taken thousands and thousands of dollars' worth of JL cattle in a year's time. If the losses continued, JL could be out of business soon.

That afternoon the JL crew was working away from headquarters and Jim Magruder was busy in his office. T. W. cut a piece of rawhide and tied his holster to his thigh, then went behind the barn to experiment with a quick draw. He analyzed the elements of what must happen to get the pistol quickly into shooting position. He tried several motions before settling on one that seemed to suit him best. The most difficult part, apart from achieving speed, was the act of pulling back the hammer with his thumb while pulling the single-action revolver out of the holster and bringing it up to pull the trigger. But he worked on it all afternoon, with an empty cylinder. He did not want to shoot himself in the foot.

By the time the men were coming in for supper, T. W. knew he could draw and shoot faster than he could before, but he would be no match for a seasoned gunslick. It would take far more than an afternoon's effort to become proficient. He planned to practice at every opportunity, in secret. If he could draw that big Colt fast enough, he might convince some adversary to keep his own gun in the holster. Had he been able to outdraw MacKenzie's gunman, Magruder and he could have finished their investigation. They might have found answers to very important questions.

That night after doing some reading, T. W. was restless. He strapped on the gunbelt and worked for a half hour in front of the large mirror that hung next to the chest of drawers. He detected several elements of his motion that needed correction. The next morning he was up early and spent another half hour watching his motion in the mirror.

He knew that drawing a gun when there was no pressure from an opponent, no threat of death, was entirely different from doing it under dire conditions of tension and danger. He thought about what Wash had said about not pulling your gun "unless you're willing to shoot it." But T. W. believed that his gun aimed at a man's belly, would be deterrent enough so that he wouldn't have to pull the trigger.

The work of the next two weeks on the JL was work every self-respecting cowman hated. Haying! Unlike many ranches in New Mexico, the JL had hay that could be cut and stored in the barn to be used in the winter, if needed. The most hateful part of the rigorous work was that it had to be done on foot. Some of the men had actually tried it on horseback but had found there was no way a man could fork hay onto the hay frame while he sat on the back of a horse. Every night the men came into the bunkhouse with sore feet, arms, and backs, and low in spirits. Although cowmen despised working on foot, they tolerated chores at roundup and branding time that could not be done on horseback because at least the men were working with cattle. Haying was farmers' work.

The JL men became irritable and quarrelsome. Chin worked especially hard to provide toothsome meals, and that did help. No matter how tired and sore T. W. was, every morning and every night he worked at least a half hour with his Peacemaker before the mirror, analyzing his draw, thumbing back the hammer and pulling the trigger when the unloaded gun was level. Every two days he cleaned and oiled the big .45. No one knew of his increased proficiency. He always practiced in secrecy and never tied down his holster except when he was practicing.

After supper of the last day of haying, T. W. asked Wash to put on his gun and come up to his room. "I want you to do me a big favor, Wash."

"If you want me to even look at a pitchfork, forget it."

"This is entirely different," T. W. said. "Take all the cartridges out of your cylinder."

"Why?"

"Come on. Just do it. I'm doing it too."

When both cylinders were empty, T. W. said, "I want to show you something. Loosen your gun in the holster. Like you were going to pull it in a hurry."

T. W. loosened his gunbelt so the holster hung low, then he tied it down with his rawhide. Wash said, "Hey, what are you doin'?"

"I just want to show you something. Now, whenever you're ready, pull your gun and pretend to shoot at me."

"I don't like this kind of game."

"Just do it once."

Wash set himself and suddenly reached for his gun. He no sooner had his hand on the walnut grips than T. W.'s pistol was leveled at his abdomen and the hammer had already clicked on the empty chamber.

"Whew, I'd be a dead man."

"What do you think?"

"You *are* fast with that thing. But . . . why are you doing this?"

"I'm hoping to be fast enough to save lives."

"Looks more like you're plannin' to end some."

"Wash, I think that if I can be this fast, I might be able to keep a few six-shooters in their holsters and prevent some people from getting killed."

"I hope it works out that way, but you might end up having to pull the trigger."

"That does worry me, but I believe I can shoot if I have to. After all, I did shoot one of the rustlers."

"Well, T. W., good luck to you."

"Wash, this is how I see it. My investigation may put me and all the JL men in dangerous situations. Whoever is organizing and carrying out this big rustling operation is in it so deep that he will not hesitate to kill. I don't want one JL man killed—I don't want anyone killed. But I do not plan to let outlaws destroy my uncle's ranch. If they are permitted to go on like they are now, it won't be long before decent people can't live in this valley."

"Every JL man will fight with you for Thad Love."

"I appreciate the deep sense of loyalty ranch hands have for their employers. You don't see that sort of thing much back East."

That night T. W. wrote to his uncle again, telling what had happened since the last letter and lavishing praise on the JL crew.

The next morning, T. W. told Jim Magruder he was going back to ride the JL-Pothook boundary again to see if there had been further suspicious trailing of cattle from JL range.

CHAPTER 11

JIM MAGRUDER WAS busy working on accounts, but he insisted T. W. take Wash Carter along on his patrol.

At the corral T. W.'s thoughts momentarily flashed back to his first morning there when Sam had bucked him off three times. That beginning of a new way of life seemed so long ago. Now he caught Sam with his first throw and he knew Sam was going to be frisky because haying had given all the riding horses a vacation. Sam pitched, crow-hopped, and twisted just as he had that first day, but now T. W. enjoyed the game and didn't even think about grabbing leather.

Another important difference was that no one watched. T. W. was another JL man, accepted by the others. He watched the men because he still had much to learn about ranch life, but he knew they would be as surprised as Wash had been if they saw how quickly he could draw his gun.

When T. W. and Wash arrived at the boundary, T. W. said, "Wash, you go north and I'll go south. But let's not go more than about a mile. We shouldn't get too far apart." When they had separated, T. W. was suddenly aware that he had given Wash an order. He had assumed command. T. W. did not feel superior to Wash in the ways of this life, but he did know what he wanted to accomplish and this was his project.

T. W. looked for a sign but did not see any. He looked back frequently at Wash. This time Wash was waving his hat; he had found something. T. W. put Sam into an easy lope. Wash had dismounted and was studying the ground.

"Twenty-five or thirty head driven along here."

"How long ago?"

"At least two weeks, about the time we started hayin' I guess. Looks like tracks of two unshod horses."

"The same old strategy."

"Unless they're real Comanches this time."

"Let's follow. See what we can see. But be alert. This is not far from where Jim and I saw that Pothook gun hand."

They came to an area where there had been branding activity. Then the cattle had been scattered. Nearby there was a small bunch grazing.

T. W. said, "Let's rope some and study them. That's what we came for."

The bunch stayed together, drifting slowly away from Wash and T. W. "Wash, they're all pretty young."

"That's so the brands will look all right by the time they're old enough to sell to a legal buyer." Wash roped a young brindle steer and both men examined it. "Any doubt in your mind, now that you've seen one up close?"

"None at all."

"In a couple weeks you couldn't prove it isn't a Pothook."

The JL men found twenty-eight cattle with altered brands and they separated them to take back to the JL. They had gone only a half mile when Wash said, "Uh-oh. Here comes trouble."

T. W. looked back. A rider was only a few hundred yards away and riding hard. "Wash, keep them moving. I'll take care of this."

It was the same two-gun Pothook man who had chased Magruder and T. W. away two weeks before. Wash pretended to do what T. W. ordered, but he was ready for action.

The gunman jerked up his horse in a cloud of dust. "Hold it right there. You're dumber than I thought, tryin' to rustle in broad daylight. Turn them cows around and start 'em back."

"These are JL cattle. Someone has changed the brand. We're taking them back as evidence for the U.S. marshal."

"You got a lot of nerve, four-eyes, I'll say that for you. Now, turn the cows back."

"We're taking them, and I'm glad you came along. We're taking you too."

"Why you—" The gunman went for his right-hand gun, but he did not have it halfway out of the holster when he saw T. W.'s Peacemaker pointed at his belt buckle, the hammer cocked. He let the gun drop back into the holster and raised both hands.

T. W. said, "Very slowly now, unbuckle your gunbelt and drop it on this side. Easy."

Wash rode up and tied the man's hands behind his back with a piggin' string he usually carried. He picked up the gunbelt and hung it on his saddle horn. The gunman did not talk as the men herded the cattle back to JL headquarters. Jim Magruder came out to see what was happening and seemed very surprised to see the cattle and the Pothook hand.

T. W. said, "We need to keep the cattle handy for evidence, Jim."

"Put them in the corral. Wash, tie up our friend in the bunkhouse."

T. W. said, "I'm going to Pothook and invite Britt MacKenzie to come over for a conference."

"You don't know the way, T. W. Shorty is mending some harness in the barn. I'll send him."

"All right, but tell him to explain nothing. I want to see Britt's face when we confront him with the evidence. We'll see how good he is at making up excuses in a hurry."

While the men at the JL waited for MacKenzie, Wash asked T. W., "What do you plan to do with him?" He nodded toward the gunman in the bunkhouse.

"Well, we have no proof of anything against him as an

individual. If MacKenzie wants him, we'll have to let him go."

"That's dangerous. You humiliated a man who makes his living by his guns. He won't forget it."

"Neither will I, Wash. Neither will I."

Wash smiled. "For an Eastern dude, you sure are startin' to cut a wide swath. Just the same, watch out for this rannie. He's the kind who will shoot you in the back if he gets a chance."

Shorty returned and reported that MacKenzie was not at Pothook headquarters, but he was supposed to be back soon and he would get the message.

Within an hour Britt MacKenzie arrived; Penelope Copeland was with him. She was wearing a light green tailored riding suit with a divided skirt. T. W. noticed how the color perfectly set off her soft auburn hair, which was mostly tucked under a white Stetson.

T. W. said, "Good afternoon, Miss Copeland. Hello, Britt."

Magruder and Wash were there and they all exchanged greetings. T. W. said, "This is an unexpected but welcome pleasure, Miss Copeland."

"Britt and I were out for an afternoon ride and I haven't been to JL headquarters for several years, so I just thought I'd ride along. The place certainly looks prosperous and well maintained."

Britt added, "Thad Love is certainly an excellent businessman and a good neighbor."

"Which brings us to the reason for our asking you to come over here."

"Well, I've certainly been wondering about your message."

"We have a very serious problem, Britt. This morning Wash and I were riding the JL-Pothook line and we saw sign that a bunch of cattle had been driven from JL to Pothook. We followed the trail, which was about two weeks old. If you will come over to the corral we'll show you what we found."

T. W. watched MacKenzie's face as he talked. There was no sign of any emotion, just a trace of puzzlement, which if feigned, was done with perfection. At the corral, Mac-Kenzie said with apparent or real surprise, "Those are Pothook cattle. Why did you bring them here?"

"Look closely, Britt. Shorty, rope one and pull it over here please."

T. W. studied Britt's face as Britt got a close look at the brand and exclaimed, "Why, that brand has been altered!" The astonishment seemed genuine. "That was a JL brand! Look at that, Penelope."

"How can you tell? It looks like a Pothook to me."

Britt explained the nature of the alteration. "The man who did this is very good with a running iron. The earmark is good, too, but that wouldn't be as hard to do."

MacKenzie turned back to the JL men. "I don't know what to say. It's obvious what has been done. It looks bad for Pothook, but surely you fellows don't think that I would order my men to rustle my neighbor's cattle."

"We don't know what to think right now, Britt. Not only about these twenty-eight, but we have to wonder how long it has been going on. How many JL cattle are wearing the Pothook or have already been trailed north?"

"It's unbelievable. I've been trying so hard to bring an end to lawlessness in the valley and now I find this sort of thing going on right under my nose."

Penelope shook her head. "I can't understand how this could happen."

T. W. studied Britt's face.

"I think I may have the solution," Britt said. "I have a bonus plan for my men. It's unusual, but I don't pay my men straight wages. I pay extra when Pothook does well. So, some of my men must have rustled your cattle to add to Pothook's trail herd to trick me into thinking they have done a far better-than-average job of keeping the screw worm under control and caring for the young calves."

Penelope seemed relieved. "That explains it. You've been too busy to properly supervise your large operation."

MacKenzie said, "I'm embarrassed. I've been taken in by my own employees. I apologize and I'll make certain it never happens again. Tomorrow I'll personally inspect my range and look for any altered brands. If I find any I'll send them back immediately and tell you about it."

T. W. said, "There is one more thing, Britt. We had some trouble this morning. One of your men tried to take back the cattle we gathered up. He even tried to use his pistol."

"Did you get his name?"

"No, but we brought him with us."

"What?"

"Wash, will you bring out our guest?"

MacKenzie berated the man thoroughly and told him to go back to Pothook. Wash handed him his gun. Shorty brought his horse and he rode off without ever saying a word, but T. W. saw the raw hate in his eyes.

T. W. invited Penelope and Britt to stay for supper, but Penelope had to direct choir practice. Several times T. W. caught her looking at him with interest.

Penelope and Britt mounted to leave and Britt apologized again. He seemed hurt when T. W. said, "I just hope it won't happen again, Britt."

T. W. felt a stirring within him when he watched Penelope ride away. She rode with a straight back and was in complete command of her spirited flaxen-maned sorrel. When the two turned past the end of the big house, Penelope looked back and returned T. W.'s wave.

"What do you think, Jim?"

"I just don't know. He certainly seemed surprised, and embarrassed."

"Ever hear of the kind of wage plan he mentioned?"

"No, I never worked under an arrangement like that."

"Wash?"

"New to me."

The next day was Saturday and the JL men rode to Yucca after baths, shaves, and exchanges of haircuts. T. W. headed for Prentice Parlors.

CHAPTER 12

T. W. RANG THE bell and George opened the door. T. W. said, "I would like to see Miss Jennifer for a few minutes, if I may."

"I don't think she's up yet, Mr. Love, but I'll see. Last night was very busy. You can wait in the living room."

It was hard to believe anyone could still be in bed at four o'clock in the afternoon, but T. W. realized that he could not comprehend the lives of Goldie's lovely doves. He waited for a half hour and was thinking he would come back later when Jennifer came into the room wearing a blue gingham afternoon dress with a close-fitting bodice and a high collar. She had piled her black hair up on her head neatly, but obviously quickly. She wore no makeup and looked rather sleepy. Pretty, nevertheless. T. W. found her languor provocative.

"Good afternoon, T. W. I wasn't expecting any gentleman callers this time of day."

"I'm sorry if I awakened you, but I did want to find out if my letter from the marshal had come yet."

"It arrived two days ago," Jennifer said and handed him the envelope.

If Jennifer noticed T. W.'s interest in her appearance, she chose to ignore it. "How have you been?" she asked brightly, making a valiant effort to get involved in the day now that she was up.

"I'm fine. How about you?"

"Just fine. I haven't seen you for weeks."

"I haven't been in town. We've been really busy with our

annual haying." T. W. laughed. "We were all so tired and sore that we went right to bed after supper every night."

"I think every man out here hates haying. I haven't heard one man say anything good about it."

T. W. did not want to think about all the men Jennifer talked to and he changed the trend of the conversation. "Have you done much riding lately?"

"Quite often, but I've taken your advice. I don't go unless George is available."

"Tomorrow is Sunday, and we don't work on Sundays at the JL unless there is a real emergency. Could we ride together?"

"I'd like to very much."

"Morning or afternoon?"

"Let's go in the late morning and I'll put together a picnic lunch for us."

"A splendid suggestion. How's eleven o'clock?"

"I'll be ready, and maybe I'll be able to surprise you with what's in the picnic basket."

Walking along the boardwalk under the wooden awnings, T. W. had some nagging reservations about the Sunday outing, even though he was looking forward to it. Was he unwise to go riding with one of the stars of the Prentice Upper Parlors? Goldie's advertisement in the weekly *Yucca Sentinel* said, "Any man will tell you." *Any man* . . . The thought was disturbing and T. W. questioned whether any of the JL men were able to afford the talented women of the upper parlor. It was unlikely. Probably only ranch owners and businessmen could buy the charms of Jennifer and the other upper-echelon women.

T. W. went to the Mercantile to buy ammunition. He had been practicing his shooting as well as continuing to work twice a day on his fast-draw artistry. Penelope Copeland was working in the store and when she saw T. W. in the gun and ammunition department she came over to talk to him. After some small talk about the weather, she put her hand on T. W.'s arm—he liked the sensation—and looked him squarely in the eyes. "You don't think Britt had anything to do with the brand changing, do you?"

It was difficult to lie to Penelope when she was so close and her eyes were searching his so intently. He groped for the right words. "I have to say I was convinced of his guilt until I talked to him, but I guess his explanation was . . . uh . . . logical. That bonus-wage plan of his is very unusual, of course."

"I'm glad you don't think he knew about the rustling."

"I'd have to believe any man who is going to marry you, because you would see through any man's dishonesty."

"Thank you for the compliment, but I want everyone to understand that Britt and I have not discussed marriage. Although most people in Yucca seem to take it for granted that we have."

"If Britt hasn't talked to you about it, he doesn't have as much sense as I've given him credit for."

"I'm the one who has refused to discuss it."

T. W. hesitated, then said, "There's something about him that worries you?"

Penelope suddenly realized she was discussing personal affairs with someone she did not know very well and she said lightly, "Oh, not at all. I believe Britt is going to be an important leader in New Mexico."

T. W. nodded. "He definitely has ambition." Then he looked directly into her eyes, challenging her to give an honest answer to the question he was about to ask. "Has Britt ever told you why he has hired those gunmen, like the one Wash and I ran into?"

"I have asked him. He said it was for protection from the Comanchero operations. That he needs them until he can convince the people here to hire a sheriff or a marshal."

"That's logical too . . . I guess."

"I know you think that Britt is hard-driving, maybe

overly ambitious. When Britt was a baby, his father died in a cholera epidemic and his mother took in washing to keep them alive. She worked herself into a case of tuberculosis and she died when he was eight. He was put in an orphanage, so you can see why he has high goals."

"Yes, but he still has to operate within the law, Penelope."

Penelope's expression was troubled.

T. W. left and walked to the Palace Saloon. Wash and Brick were leaning on the bar, studying the large painting of the voluptuous reclining blond.

Brick said, "Once in a while I think it would be good to be a family man. Have a woman around all the time. It sure would have its advantages."

Wash said, "Don't forget all the disadvantages. All the responsibilities, children under foot and yellin', no more footloose and fancy free, no more going over the next hill to see what's on the other side."

T. W. laughed, then he called out, "Heinie, two of the same for my friends and a sarsaparilla for me." Heinie set down the drinks and T. W. said, "Wash wants to know why no saloon has a painting of a black woman hanging behind the bar. You know a good reason?"

Heinie fingered his splendidly curled mustache thoughtfully. "I don't rightly know, but if someone finds a good one, I'll put her up there, too."

"There you are, Wash," T. W. said. "All we have to do is find one. If we can't, I'll commission one—if I ever have enough money."

Wash snorted. "Promises."

T. W. picked up his sarsaparilla and said, "I'm going to a table. When you two get through mooning, come over and join me."

He opened his letter. The marshal had been thorough in his inquiries. There was a listing of people with large deposits in every bank in northern New Mexico. He had made marginal notations indicating that most of the people were owners of large ranches and their deposits were in line with the size of their operations. Britt MacKenzie had a large deposit in Yucca, but it was not unusually large considering the size of the Pothook. Jim Magruder, though, had ten thousand dollars in his deposit. T. W. almost wished he had not seen that entry.

Maybe Magruder had inherited some money. He surely could not have saved that much in the years since the war, not from his wages as a foreman on the JL. T. W. reminded himself that Jim never drank or gambled and that he had never seen him come to town on Saturday. Still, that was a lot of money. A heck of a lot of money, and it added one more facet to the mystery. And there was no way he could find out whether Britt or Jim had other accounts under fictitious names in banks somewhere else.

What should the next move be? Ride over to the Pecos and investigate the Comancheros? He might find something that would either clearly establish the guilt of Britt and Jim or clear them of suspicion. He put the letter in his pocket and soon Wash and Brick joined him. They watched the men around them playing poker, blackjack, and monte. Shorty and Duke were beating the dealer at blackjack and soon they came to the table to brag about their skill.

Brick said, "If you keep playin,' you'll lose it all back, so let's go get some vittles before you do."

After steak, fried potatoes, coffee, and big wedges of dried-apple pie, most of the JL men drifted off in pursuit of other pleasures. Wash saw a copy of *The New Mexican* on a table recently vacated by another group. "Let's see if there's anything new in the Territory. Uh-oh. Listen to this: 'Last night four inmates were broken out of the Santa Fe jail in a daring raid. The escaped men are the fake Comanches apprehended several weeks ago while rustling cattle from Thad Love's ranch near Yucca. Any information about them will be appreciated by the marshal.' That's bad news, T. W."

"Bad news indeed."

"That skinny one will be looking for revenge, especially against you, since you're the one who put the lead in his shoulder."

"Wash, I wonder how much MacKenzie knows about all this."

"You know that by this time, if he's actually in this Comanchero operation, he's figured out that you've become a problem he has to get rid of. And if he *is* in this, he won't have to do any persuading to set those four galoots on your trail. And then there's that two-gun hombre we had trouble with the other day. He's gonna be lookin' for you too. You've suddenly got a passel of people huntin' for you."

"Yes, I understand the situation, but you know, this may work to our advantage."

"I don't see how."

"Somebody is bound to show his hand soon because we're threatening his operation and he's not sure just how much we know. If we could capture one of the subordinates, we might be able to get some information."

"Well, I'm more worried about keeping you alive than capturing anybody. You've got to have one of us with you every time you leave headquarters."

"No, Wash, there's no need for any JL man to risk his life. This is between me and whoever is going to try to stop me."

"Now listen to me. Carefully. You've learned more in a short time about punchin' cows than anybody I've ever seen. But there's an awful lot you still don't know about this country and how to stay alive in it. There's no honor or decency in the men who are your enemies. Now that they've found out how fast you are with your Peacemaker, none of them will face you in a fair fight. They'll shoot you in the back. Besides all that, you don't know how to track or read sign very well. You don't know the places where they can ambush you. You don't know your way around in the mountains. You don't—"

"Hold it. Hold it. I guess there's a lot of truth in what you are saying, but I know enough to get along. And I'll tell you, Wash, the whole JL is not worth the death of even one of our crew. So, I'm the one who's going to take whatever risks are involved."

Wash and T. W. walked back to the Palace and T. W. chose a table in the corner where no one could come up behind him.

Wash laughed and said, "You're learnin', but sittin' in the Palace is a lot different than bein' out on the range or walkin' down one of Yucca's streets at night."

Wash went to sit in on a poker game with some men he knew from other ranches. T. W. watched the saloon women in action, dancing and drinking with the customers. He saw the difference in class between them and the Prentice Parlors women. Most of these women were coarse, heavily rouged, older, and wore garish low-cut dresses. Was this the fate of Prentice girls who had lost the bloom, unless some cattleman married them?

He thought about Jennifer. She might be with a client right at this moment. He was torturing himself with this train of thought, but he couldn't stop thinking about Jennifer Prentice. He liked to be with her. He was at ease when he was with her, but then she could probably put any man at ease. *Any man.*

Wash left his poker game and sat down with T. W. "Win or lose, Wash?"

"Winner, but not by much. I found out other people are losin' cattle, in small bunches, but regularly. All the trails lead east. The punchers I was talkin' to think they go to the Pecos."

"Maybe across Pothook?"

"Sometimes, but not always."

"Are there many brands that could be changed to a Pothook?"

"Quite a few . . ."

"So Britt could keep those, fatten them up, and trail them north after a few months. The others he could take right over to the river."

"Right."

"It's got to be MacKenzie. Wash, I'm going to put him behind bars."

"Sounds good. All you need is proof."

"I'll get it, Wash. I *will* get it."

The next morning was Sunday and the cowhands were enjoying their once-a-week late rising time. T. W. caught Sam and quietly rode out just as the sun was about to ease above the horizon. He thought no one knew, but Chin heard him and went to the bunkhouse to tell Wash.

"Damn it, Chin. He's goin' to get himself killed riding off alone."

CHAPTER 13

WASH DRESSED, THEN rode out after T. W. He caught up with him halfway to Yucca, because T. W. was holding Sam to walking and easy loping. Wash kept him almost always in sight. He figured T. W. would not be watching his backtrail. It just would not occur to him to do it. Easy prey for a backshooter.

T. W. rode down Main street through Yucca to the church, which was built out on the edge of town to be away from the saloons. His picnic with Jennifer was not for a few hours but he had come to town early in the hope of getting a glimpse of Penelope directing the choir.

Some saddled horses and horses hitched to buckboards stood at the hitching racks, and a few townsfolk were walking up to the door of the white clapboard building with its small bell tower.

T. W. sat down in the back row and watched people find places to sit. There were several family groups, mostly town people, although some appeared to be ranching families. There were just a few single men and women in the congregation. Britt soon came in alone. He walked down the aisle and sat next to a family group, exchanging greetings with those around him. He had not seen T. W.

The choir came in through a side door and sat on benches behind the handmade pulpit. Penelope followed the singers and went to the piano, placed so she could direct them. She was wearing a white summery dress with a close-fitting bodice that emphasized her bosom, whether she intended for it to do so or not. Her auburn hair was carefully swept up and T. W. imagined the soft beauty of it if she were to let it cascade over her shoulders.

As they sang, T. W. tried to match each voice with a singer, but gave up that diversion and soon found he enjoyed the well-trained singing of Penelope's eight women and five men. She played the piano accompaniment for the choir, and with authority and vigor she set the tempo to carry along the congregation's hymn singing. After the singing, she sat facing the congregation, smiling. As her gaze swept the rows of faces of friends, neighbors, and customers, it was almost as though she were bestowing a kind of benevolent, "all-is-forgiven" smile. Her smile broadened when she looked at MacKenzie and gave way briefly to slight puzzlement when she saw T. W. She recovered quickly and fastened her attention on the burly, bearded minister, who held the attention of everyone as he preached a fervent fire-and-brimstone sermon.

Penelope and the choir led the enthusiastic singing of the last hymn and T. W. slipped out quickly before all the handshaking at the door began.

He was surprised to see Wash across the street, sitting in the shade of his horse. T. W. crossed over to him and said, "Hey, you missed a good sermon. What are you doing here?"

"Well, there's this fellow from Boston who apparently thinks the bad men aren't bad on Sunday. He rides alone for ten miles and doesn't check his backtrail to see if anybody's following him. I doubt if he was doin' any serious lookin' in front of him either."

"So that's what it's all about. All right, I was careless. I admit it. But what are you doing here?"

"I came to keep an eye on you. By the way, I didn't know you had religion."

"I don't know whether I have it, Wash, but I attend church quite regularly back in Boston and I just got to wondering what a service would be like here in Yucca."

"What did you find out?"

"Not so formal here, but the same idea."

"Ready to go back to the JL now?"

"Actually, I won't be going back until late this afternoon. I've arranged to take Jennifer Prentice for a ride this afternoon. She's putting together some food for a picnic."

"You can't ride around by yourself. You'll get yourself shot in the back. I'll go along."

"Wash, you know very well that three is an awkward number for a picnic of this sort."

Wash finally said he would go back to the JL after he had some breakfast. T. W. ate with him, then they sat around in the Palace until time for T. W. to meet Jennifer.

George opened the door. In a low voice he said, "You take care of Miss Jennifer, Mr. Love. You may not know it, but there are men who want to kill you. I tried to persuade Miss Jennifer it isn't safe for her to ride with you, but she says you'll protect her."

With a good-natured smile, T. W. said, "I'll do my best, George."

When Jennifer walked down the staircase, she wore a powder blue tailored suit with a divided skirt, a small cameo at the collar of her white blouse, and a low-crowned, wide-brimmed hat for protection from the sun.

George brought her horse around, a fine-featured chestnut filly with long mane and tail and intelligent eyes. T. W. was surprised to see that Jennifer was going to ride sidesaddle. It just wasn't Western, but nothing about Jennifer's appearance was Western except for the hat.

T. W. put the food packages in their saddlebags. Then he helped Jennifer mount.

Jennifer was gay and talkative. Her eyes sparkled and she laughed easily. She sat her saddle expertly and handled her pretty little filly with an easy competence. T. W. asked if she knew a place for their picnic and she said she knew just the place. They headed east toward the hazy, blue Sangre de Cristo range. The usual July afternoon thundershowers had greened some of the vegetation and here and there the tall yucca spears still retained their delicate, creamy flowers.

Jennifer pointed to a yucca and asked, "Do you know what that is?"

"I think it's yucca, but some of the JL men call it soapweed."

"It's also called Spanish Bayonet, but the name I like best of all is God's Candle."

Odd that she should favor a name like God's Candle. Perhaps some remnant of her upbringing. Or maybe she didn't consider her occupation to be sinful—what she did with her body was separate from her soul.

Jennifer suggested they canter. They rode together without talking until they slowed to a walk again. T. W. was trying to remember to be alert for a possible ambush and he even looked back sometimes. He never saw anything anywhere to disturb the pleasure of riding with Jennifer.

She said, "See the trees ahead? That's the spot."

"There must be a river." He laughed and added, "I've learned that much about the valley."

There had been rain and a small rivulet ran slowly through a shallow watercourse. The grass was tall and green and there was a coolness under the cottonwoods.

"How is this?" Jennifer asked.

"Just perfect."

He helped Jennifer dismount and he was not at all surprised at the surge in his heartbeat as their bodies momentarily came together. But Jennifer gave no indication that she had a similar sensation.

Brightly she said, "Hand me the saddlebags and I'll set up our lunch."

T. W. staked the horses and Jennifer spread a dark red tablecloth on the grass. She filled two plates with sandwiches and golden fried chicken. She opened a small walnut box and withdrew a small wine bottle and two diminutive stemmed wine glasses.

T. W. immediately decided this was an occasion to warrant the drinking of an alcoholic beverage. Jennifer poured a cool, flavorful, white wine into the glasses, raised hers, and said, "Here's to a beautiful day."

"To a beautiful day and a beautiful lady."

There was light, witty conversation, sometimes about books, sometimes about the Estancia Valley and the town of Yucca. When they had eaten the food and drunk the wine in their glasses, T. W. asked, "Is there a little wine left in that bottle?"

"About two swallows," Jennifer said and poured.

"I'd like to propose a toast," T. W. said, and lifted his glass. "To a lovely, charming lady who has provided a day I shall never forget."

They drank the wine and Jennifer said, "I'll remember the happiness of this day for a very long time."

They were close enough for him to bend forward and kiss her, but she leaned back, still smiling at him but just out of reach.

He held her eyes with his and she did not waver. "Jennifer, what is a beautiful, well-educated, desirable . . ."

She raised her hand to stop him. "Don't," she said softly. Don't ask me that. Don't spoil our wonderful adventure."

Then she stood up, assumed a contrived gaiety, and began packing things into the saddlebags. T. W. brought the horses and tied the saddlebags on them. Jennifer put on her hat and said, "Sidesaddles are so hard to get up on. Would you be so kind as to help a lady?"

"Certainly, my pleasure." He placed his hands around her small waist and she looked up at him. He took her head in his hands, and gently pressed his lips softly to hers. Suddenly her body became rigid and she stepped back.

She looked at him squarely and said, "Stop it. I could never be what you want. I know myself too well. I couldn't be a rancher's wife. Or a banker's wife, or anyone's wife. And you could never accept what I am, what I've been." There was no bitterness or remorse in her voice. "I like my life. My days are my own to do with as I please. I read, paint, play my piano. Do just whatever I want to do. I have my own money, and I have a growing account in a St. Louis bank for when . . . for when I'm older."

"But . . . ," T. W. began.

With a big smile, she said, "Help me up, please. We've had a lovely picnic. Now, let's ride like the wind."

She put her filly into a gallop and T. W. had to ride hard to catch her. He would like to ride up, take her from the saddle, and whisk her off to Boston, to a new life. But as much as he hated to admit it, he knew she was right, especially about him. Pushing the thought from his mind, he pressed his horse harder to catch up with Jennifer.

Just as he was pulling even with her, T. W. heard the whine of a bullet well above them, then the bark of a rifle from somewhere in front. Jennifer looked at him and he motioned for her to keep riding, straight ahead. He had looked back. Four men were riding hard toward them. Only about a quarter mile behind. Ahead were Wash and George in an arroyo, visible only from the shoulders up. They were firing at the pursuers. Several wild shots came from behind them. Jennifer and T. W. rode into the arroyo and T. W. helped Jennifer to the ground. "Stay low," he said. George led the filly to safety and T. W. jerked his rifle from the scabbard and went to the rim of the arroyo. The four men had stopped just outside of rifle range and were talking. Soon they turned and withdrew. Four rifles against three were not good enough odds. Wash watched them go. T. W. went to Jennifer.

"Are you all right?"

"I'm fine, but my heart is sure beating fast. That's the first time I've ever been shot at."

"I'm sorry, Jennifer. It's my fault. I should have listened to George and Wash. They warned me but I really didn't think there was any danger." T. W. turned to Wash. "How did you two happen to be here?"

"Well, we didn't just happen to be here. We've been here all afternoon. We decided we'd better follow you, just in case."

George added, "Just as you were leaving, those four showed up and started chasing you. They didn't shoot at first because they knew they would catch you soon."

Wash said, "If they had gotten closer, we would have ridden out instead of waitin' here."

"Well, thank you for pulling my fat out of the fire. Without you two it would have been a very serious predicament for us." Then he turned to Jennifer. "My stubborn naïveté almost cost you your life. I'm really sorry."

At Prentice Parlors, George took the chestnut filly to the stable and T. W. walked Jennifer to the door. He took her hand and said, "I feel awful about what happened."

"I'm just as much to blame," she said. "George warned me. But I wanted a small, nostalgic taste of my old life in St. Louis. You gallantly provided it and I thank you."

The two JL men rode west toward the ranch. The sun was going down behind the Jemez range. The lofty white cumulus clouds that had been gathering all afternoon were dispersing and the golds and pinks and reds of those clouds were fascinating to T. W.

"What a country, Wash. All this indescribable beauty, this great, spacious, colorful land."

"You know, you're a funny maverick. I'll speak right out. You nearly got yourself killed because of your carelessness, and here you are, ridin' along like you don't have a care in the world. Just starin' at the sky."

"I've always been kind of taken in by great sunsets. But

I've learned my lesson, Wash. I'll be watching the trail like a hawk."

Neither man spoke until T. W. asked, "Do you think those men were the gang that escaped from prison?"

"It's hard to be sure at a quarter mile, but I think so."

"And MacKenzie was so pious this morning at church."

"He's got almost everybody fooled, even Penelope Copeland."

"I'm not so sure of that, Wash. I don't think she completely swallowed his explanation about our steers with the Pothook brand on them. She wants to believe it, but I think she has some doubts."

T. W. forced himself to be observant. It had to become a habit, this scanning the backtrail, looking from side to side, listening for sounds that shouldn't be there. It must be his way from now until the head Comanchero was caught and his crew of killers were behind bars or dead. Or, possibly, until he, T. W. Love, was dead.

CHAPTER 14

AFTER SUPPER T. W. asked Wash to come to his room in the big adobe. Wash sat down and looked around. "You sure read a lot," he said when he saw the stack of books on the chest of drawers.

"I read every night for an hour or so. If you see any that look good to you, you're welcome to borrow them."

"I might just take you up on that sometime soon. I'm gettin' tired of readin' old newspapers and labels on Chin's canned goods."

"Wash, I've made a decision."

"I don't like the sound of that. What is it?"

"I'm going into enemy territory."

"Meanin' what?"

"I'm going to the Pecos, and somehow I'm going to get the evidence that will connect Britt with the Comanchero operation. I'm convinced he's the leader of it all."

"If he is, why is he messin' around with the penny ante stuff like takin' JL steers?"

"Remember, Wash, all the penny ante stuff adds up to a big pot. I think MacKenzie is too greedy and in too big of a hurry. He's gotten careless and I think I can catch him in his next mistake."

"When do we leave? Tonight?"

"Sorry, but this is a mission you can't volunteer for. I really appreciate your offer to go with me, but I can't accept it."

"Let's not go through all this again. You're not ready to take care of yourself out here. You'll be dead before you get across the Sangres."

"I won't allow a JL man to endanger his life on such a dangerous expedition."

Wash allowed a long sigh to escape. "If you say I can't go, this is what I'm goin' to do—go to Magruder and quit my job. I won't be a JL man any longer and you can't give me any orders. Then I'll just follow along behind you. You can't keep a man from goin' where he wants to go."

"Wash . . ."

"Another thing, I've kinda taken a likin' to you, and I don't want to bury your bones after the vultures have finished with your carcass."

T. W. looked down at the floor momentarily, then he said, "Wash, you're the truest friend I've ever had. I guess I can't stop you. I'll tell Magruder. Let's leave as soon as it gets dark."

"Good. I'll go and get Chin to put us up some trail grub."

Magruder tried to dissuade T. W. from the mission. "It's just plain too dangerous, T. W. I feel responsible for you while you're here. I think your uncle would agree that this is too risky. And I know he would rather have you return to Boston alive than in a box. The cows aren't that important to Thad Love."

"I understand, Jim, but I've made up my mind."

"But T. W., you're such a . . . a . . ."

T. W. smiled. "Greenhorn, Jim?"

"I guess that's what I was goin' to say," Magruder replied. "Well, T. W., I don't approve but I can't stop you. I hope you find what you're looking for and come back in one piece."

When Wash and T. W. rode by the house, lamplight came from Magruder's office window. T. W. thought about Magruder's large bank account. Was his attempt to stop this mission a real concern or an attempt to prevent the

search for evidence? The time had come to find out. One
way or the other.

The two had been on the trail for about an hour when
T. W. pulled Sam to a stop and said, "Listen. . . . Hear
anything?"

After several minutes, Wash said, "No, I don't. Do you?"

"No, I was wondering whether someone was following
us."

"Someone from the JL?"

"Not necessarily, but I still don't know about Magruder.
If he should be in this operation, it would be smart for
him to get rid of me as soon as possible."

"I'm bettin' on Jim. And I'll tell you somethin' else.
There's not a single JL man who would double-cross Thad
Love."

"I think you're right. I sure hope so, but I've read too
often about criminal cases where people were simply'
astounded at the guilt of someone they had trusted completely."

"Well, I'm puttin' my money on the whole JL bunch."

T. W. would reserve judgment until all the facts were
known. And as they rode, he went over in his mind every
man in the crew. He could find no reason to suspect a
single one, except Magruder.

With the dark came the stars and about midnight the
moon rose above the mountains. They could see better
and make better time, but the moon's brightness lessened
the brilliance of the stars that covered the sky. From his
first night in New Mexico T. W. had marveled at the night
skies. In Boston the stars—what ones you could see—were
dim. Here they were bright, seemed much closer, and you
couldn't begin to count them.

The trail began to climb and the piñons became more
numerous. Soon the ascent was steeper and the horses
breathed harder.

"Wash, should we be resting our horses, and ourselves?"

"Yep. I've been lookin' for a good place."

They descended into a dry watercourse and Wash said, "Let's try this. There's a little grass in case the horses want to graze."

"Let's tether them and take off the saddles so they'll rest better."

T. W. couldn't see Wash's smile of approval, and the two lay down with their saddles for pillows. T. W. awoke just as the dawn was beginning to silhouette the highest peaks. He shook his boots to make certain that nothing had crawled in during the dark hours. The dew had dampened his socks and it was hard to pull his boots on over them. He walked out of the arroyo and looked for sign of any other riders. Keeping to cover, he soon found that in the dark they had crossed the trail of at least a hundred head of steers. The trail was maybe three days old.

When he returned to the arroyo, Wash was struggling with his boots and T. W. told him what he had found. They saddled up and rode back to the trail. Wash agreed with T. W.'s reading of the sign. He asked, "How many riders did you figure were pushin' this herd?"

"I forgot about that. But I'm better than I used to be."

"Yeah, in a few more years you'll probably be able to take care of yourself."

After further study, T. W. said, "The horses were un-shod, as usual, and there were four of them. Right?"

"You're learnin'."

"Is there another way across the mountains? This trail seems to be well traveled. It seems like we might meet some people we don't want to meet yet."

"There's another way. It's longer but I agree that we better take it."

They stayed among the trees and off the ridges. T. W. kept his eyes moving, searching the rocks above them and the canyon below, making himself concentrate on what was necessary for survival and success. At noon they stopped in a small box canyon with a narrow opening to a beautiful meadow with tall grass up to the horses' bellies. They let the horses rest and graze close by while they ate some of Chin's trail grub.

T. W. said, "If you keep an eye on the situation here, I'll climb a little higher and look around with my binoculars."

"Be careful."

T. W. returned. "Maybe we're going to have a little excitement."

"What did you see?"

"Nothing definite, but twice I saw the sun reflect off something shiny. It was a fleeting kind of thing."

"On our backtrail?"

"Yes."

"How far back?"

"I'd guess three, maybe four, miles. There's nothing natural around here to reflect the sun, is there? It would have to come from a gunbarrel or a silver decoration on a saddle or bridle."

"We better move on. There might be one man—or a dozen."

"One thing is certain, Wash. Whoever is back there could make better time lower down and have easier going. So it's someone who doesn't want to be seen or it's someone following our trail. Either way it's a problem."

They saddled up and rode. The trail was soon narrower, steeper, rockier, and more dangerous. They often dismounted and led the horses. The air was thinner and breathing became difficult for horses and men. In some places the trail was only a few feet wide, with a wall of rock on one side and a precipice on the other. They stopped often and rested.

Finally the trail started to descend but it was no less treacherous and in many places they felt safer when they led the horses.

T. W. said, "Let's stop for a minute and discuss strategy—as soon as there's a good place."

They came to a wider area and stopped. Wash asked, "What kind of strategy are we talkin' about?"

"It seems to me we have a choice of two courses of action. We can go on down the mountain and find a place for defense. Or we can get off the trail as soon as we can find a good place where it's still rocky and we won't leave a sign."

"Let them go by?"

"Then we could follow them instead."

"If they figure they had lost our trail, and they're goin' to report to the head Comanchero, they might lead us right to him."

"That's a good possibility as I see it. It wouldn't do us any good to ambush them up here, because I don't know what we'd do with them if we did capture them."

"Well, I vote for lettin' them go by. How about you?"

"Sounds good to me."

Wash found a good place to get off the trail, and they led their horses up a sharp incline solid enough to show no evidence of what they had done. They hid behind some large rocks about two hundred feet from the trail leading down to the Pecos, still miles away. They ate some hardtack and jerky, and T. W. admired the high-altitude beauty around him. Scrub oak, mountain mahogany, and tall ponderosas were scattered among the outcroppings and boulders. Not far above them was the timberline and above that only short-stemmed alpine plants grew.

They heard the riders before they saw them. Slim was in the lead when they came around a sharp bend, with the rest of the murderous bunch following closely. They were concentrating on the perilous footing for their horses and passed on by. Soon Wash and T. W. could not hear them anymore.

"Wash, how long should we wait before we go on?"

"Let me ask you a question. If you were Slim and couldn't find our tracks when you got down to soft ground, what would you do?"

"I'd spend some time cutting for our trail."

"And when you didn't find it?"

"Hm. That's a good question. Would I come back up the trail? Or would I go to the Comanchero rendezvous?" After more thought, T. W. said, "I don't know how smart this Slim is, but I think I would decide that we had not come over the mountain after all—that we had misled him on the other side, had started up the trail, then left it, and let them go by."

"That's the way I figure it. It's too late in the day to start back over the pass, so they'll either camp tonight and come back in the morning, or decide to go to their rendezvous."

"So we'd better wait for a couple of hours and give them enough daylight to get off the mountain."

They had been sitting for some time with their backs against the rocks when Wash said, "I don't like to keep harpin' on the same subject, but just you remember—if you pull that Colt out of the holster, plan on pullin' the trigger while you're alive to pull it."

"I know these men are desperate. I won't forget it."

CHAPTER 15

THE SUN WAS setting behind them and T. W. had ample time to admire the scene around him. It was only the second time he had been in the mountains and had the chance to really study their craggy beauty. He thought of the many natural settings that could really cast a spell over a man. The oceans could be serene and woo a man into philosophical reveries, or they could challenge his right to live with their mountainous waves and raging winds. The great north woods could make a man wonder what the oldest trees had seen, and make him humble, and make him sorry to see the mighty giants crash to the earth when man cut them down. But these mountains, these grand upthrusts from out of the earth, never changed and yet were always changing as the sun traveled over them altering their colors and moods. In late afternoon the sun painted some red here and some pink there; and dabbed some dark blue next to some purple. T. W. could watch the panorama every morning and every night and never tire of the watching.

When it was time to leave, he had to force himself back to the reality and danger of his mission, to the larger purpose he was trying to achieve.

It was dark when they rode down off the mountain into a thick stand of piñons. They had miscalculated how long it would take to get down there, so it was too dark to look for Slim and the others. Neither man liked the turn of events. They moved away from the trail to where there was some grass for the horses and settled down to another fireless camp—more hardtack and jerky.

T. W. volunteered to take the first watch. Wash was quickly asleep and T. W. sat with his back against a rock and his Winchester across his knees. He was not accustomed to nights in the open. He heard noises he had never noticed before and they all seemed louder than they should be. He told himself that all the sounds were natural ones made by nocturnal animals and birds making their nightly search for food. Then a twig snapped and he slipped his finger around the Winchester's trigger.

If someone was out there—to his right—he wanted to give no sign that he had been alerted. Hardly turning his head, he searched through the darkness. Nothing he could see. He heard no movement. The horses were to his left. Wash was about ten feet in front of him in a slight depression. If a man was out there he could not see Wash. Only the stars alleviated the darkness among the trees and T. W. could see nothing. He tried to think of a night animal heavy enough to break a large twig. There were some all right, but they usually steered clear of humans.

If he heard another sound out there he would take the rifle in his left hand, throw himself to the left, draw his pistol while in the air, and fire as soon as he landed. Then he would roll two more times and fire again. He did not know whether that was good tactically, but it seemed to be all he could do. He would be moving toward the horses, and that was vitally important. To lose their mounts would be the same as signing their death warrants.

Slim must have seen them come off the mountain and had waited until dark to attack. He and Wash were probably surrounded, but Slim's bunch couldn't see any better than they could. T. W. wanted to warn Wash, but Wash would know what was happening as soon as the first shot was fired.

There was no more sound. It was a war of nerves. Five minutes passed and T. W. knew someone was out there because all the natural nocturnal sounds had ceased. Finally he heard a small stone move against another one.

He tightened his grip on the rifle. He started his move at the same instant he heard a pistol shot and a hot pain seared its way across his right forearm. He landed and fired in the direction of the sound and rolled quickly. Another shot and a bullet hit the earth where he had just been. He aimed at the point of flame and heard a curse. He had hit somebody. T. W. rolled again and fired. No curse from that spot, but a shot rang out from below.

Wash answered that one with his rifle. A shot came from up above, to the left. A bullet ricocheted off a rock and whined off into the night.

T. W. did not try to answer that one. He had rolled into a small depression and did not want to give away his position. He was watching for another telltale spot of flame. When none appeared, he felt his forearm. There was warm blood. He explored carefully. It was a superficial wound. He could bend his fingers and rotate his wrist. He wouldn't lose much blood but it felt like somebody had drawn a hot poker across his skin.

He put his mind back on their predicament. He and Wash were about twenty feet apart and could not communicate. Any sound would bring a probing shot and it might be a lucky one. The one good thing was that the outlaws could not communicate either. Slim had made a mistake by waiting until complete dark. He should have attacked just before it got so dark or he should have waited until the moon rose and provided some light.

Apparently that was what Slim was going to do now. No one moved for a long time. T. W. began to worry about the horses. There had been one shot from someone in that direction. Slim would not let them keep their horses; one of the outlaws was probably there now, quietly trying to untether them. They were fifty feet away and T. W. started toward them. He crawled slowly, handicapped by his rifle, moving each arm and leg separately, feeling the ground ahead of him for twigs and stones that would give away his location. He kept his head up, searching for any shadowy form that did not belong where it was. He could hear the horses and knew he was close. They were nervous and were moving restlessly, so most likely someone was there.

He continued to try to see, but all shapes blended into each other. Then he suddenly remembered what an old mariner had told him about seeing at night. Look a little above what you want to see because something about the anatomy of the eye made the image register if you did not look directly at it. He raised his line of vision a little and scanned the area. He hesitated when he detected a foreign shape. Trying hard to see it, he looked right at it and it disappeared. He forced himself to look above it and it registered again. It was a man. No doubt. No features were distinguishable, just the dark bulk.

T. W. forced himself to keep his eyes focused above the figure. It moved one step closer to the horses, then waited about a minute before taking the next cautious step. T. W. slowly raised his rifle and tried to sight in on the bulk, but when he looked down the barrel, the figure disappeared.

When T. W. saw him again the man was nearly at the head of one of the horses. T. W. had to shoot or risk being trapped there. T. W. squeezed the trigger and the hulk spun around, then fell heavily to the ground. He was alive—T. W. could hear him swearing—but he did not try to go anywhere.

T. W. checked on the man, who was sitting up and holding his shoulder. T. W. shoved the rifle against his back and removed the man's revolver. There were no other firearms, but he had a long-bladed knife in a sheath under his arm. T. W. took the lariat the outlaw had dropped and tied his hands and feet behind his back. Then he took the man's bandanna and pressed it against the bullet wound to slow the loss of blood.

"If you don't move around," he said, "this will stay in position, otherwise you're going to lose an awful lot of blood. Probably bleed to death."

There was no response, and T. W. moved away slowly and quietly. He sat down to decide what he should do. He had often heard that the best defense was a good offense. That certainly fit his situation. There were three men left and they would not try to get to the horses since the shot left them wondering what had happened. T. W. started back, on hands and knees again, inching his way down the slope toward the man who was below Wash. He continued looking above the level he wanted to see. In twenty minutes he figured he was in the vicinity and moved with even greater deliberation.

His arm burned and throbbed with pain. Every time he put weight on it, the hot stab shot up into his shoulder. But he had played rugby with the pain of bruised and strained muscles. He could stand physical agony. There was satisfaction that came with carrying on despite it. So again, he told himself to wipe away the anguish from his consciousness and concentrate on the problem confronting him. Between each move and the next one T. W. continued the search with his eyes. Find the dark shape that does not belong. At last, he saw someone off to his left. Whoever it was lay on his belly, facing the position where Wash was probably still holding out.

T. W. moved so he could come up behind the man. Each move was made with even greater care. If he could get close enough, he could use the long barrel of his Peacemaker on the back of the man's head. When he was only five feet from the man, T. W. lay down his rifle and drew his pistol. Then he launched himself and landed with his knees on the man's back, driving the breath out of him with a great rush of air. T. W. hit him behind the ear with his gun barrel.

T. W. had feared Wash might shoot toward all the

commotion, but the ranch hand had held his fire. T. W. remained motionless, then heard rapid movement to his right, with no care taken to be quiet. He heard Wash fire a couple of shots in that direction. T. W. heard the whine of both bullets and knew neither had hit anything. One of the bushwhackers had escaped.

"Wash," T. W. said in a stage whisper, "I'm coming up to you."

"Come ahead."

When he reached Wash, T. W. said, "I've got one up near the horses, wounded and tied up. The one down from here is unconscious. I laid my gun barrel back of his ear. Another one is above us and he's wounded, but I don't know how badly."

"They taught you a lot at Harvard. You've done a good night's work."

"What shall we do now?"

"I think I better ask you. You've done it all so far."

"How about this? You tie up the one I just knocked out and I'll go check on the condition of the first one."

"Good enough, General," Wash said amicably.

The moon was not yet visible, but there was a little light from it already. T. W. found the one who had started the whole chain of events when he snapped the twig. He was dead.

Wash came up. "How about this one?"

"He's dead."

Wash knew T. W.'s thinking. "Now listen, you can't feel guilty about killin' this gunman. He was tryin' to kill you. What you did was plain self-defense."

"I know you're right. I just wish it hadn't turned out this way."

"Say, does that rannie over by the horses go by the name of Slim?"

"Unfortunately, no."

"Then Slim was the one runnin' off. What are we gonna do with these jaspers?"

"We can't take them with us. Let's just leave them here and come back later."

"Fine. Maybe a grizzly will come by and chomp on 'em a little. Save everybody a lot of trouble. We can just put their guns under a rock someplace."

"Let's take them with us. Maybe we'll find them handy."

"Good. Say, you up to all this? You haven't had any rest yet."

"I don't have nerves of steel like you Westerners do. I couldn't possibly sleep."

"Ready to look for that rendezvous then? It's pretty light now. I think we can find Slim's trail."

The moon rose above the Sangre de Cristo range and provided enough light to see Slim's tracks. He had taken the other three horses, gone down to the valley floor, and headed north. About a mile along he had left the river and gone up the slope into the piñons. T. W. and Wash rode cautiously. They found where Slim had tied the three horses he was leading. He headed north again, angling back toward the river.

"Why is he doing that, Wash?"

"The trail along the river gets real narrow, with high bluffs on each side. It's like that for about three miles. He couldn't lead those horses through there, and I was wonderin' what he was goin' to do."

"The cattle trail the rustlers use must come out not very far beyond the canyon, then."

"A couple of miles. The valley widens out plenty and they could hold a couple thousand head there for a short time while they bring in small bunches. Then they'd push 'em north to the railroad."

"Will we get there before dawn?"

"It'll be close."

"Can Slim ambush us in the canyon?"

"I don't see how. The walls are straight up."

They had to ride single file. Three weeks earlier, the Pecos, fed by snowmelt from higher up, would have covered this part of the trail, hurtling over the rocks, white-foamed, wild, and beautiful. It was still a rushing torrent, not as wide as it had been, but no one could stay alive if he fell into it. T. W. stayed up close behind Wash until the trail widened, then rode alongside in silence. T. W. remembered what Brick had said to him after the fight with Big John Oates: "You'll do to ride the river with."

T. W. was applying that Western saying to Wash. He could not think of one friend he had in Boston who would endanger his own life to go on such a wildly conceived expedition as this one. He had good friends back there, staunch friends, but they would have told T. W. to report the situation to the authorities and would have refused to accompany him. But Wash was different. In fact, Brick, Duke, Shorty, all would have come with him, out of loyalty to the JL.

T. W. did not put Jim Magruder in the same category. He hoped to put his suspicions to rest soon. Whatever was uncovered would surely implicate Britt MacKenzie. T. W. regretted what MacKenzie's guilt might do to Penelope Copeland, but she would recover. There was steel in her, beneath the auburn hair, the green eyes, and the softness. A woman to "ride the river with" if there ever was one.

The canyon leveled out very suddenly and Wash took them off the trail, up the piñon-juniper slope where there was good cover. Picking their way cautiously, they stopped frequently to listen. Once they heard a man singing, the time-honored method for soothing restless cattle. They dismounted and walked. The Pecos took a turn to the east and left a large flood plain between itself and the mountains.

"Look at that," Wash said. "There must be twenty-five hundred longhorns down there."

"That's a lot of money at the railroad. A lot of other people's money."

"Some JL money there too."

"They must be about to start up the trail."

"They have to move 'em out. The grass wouldn't last long with that many steers."

"Wash, how many men will it take to handle a herd this size?"

"I see six soogans down there around the fire, and there must be three men on night herd. That's nine against two."

"Not the best of odds, Wash."

CHAPTER 16

"ALL RIGHT, WASH. We're here and we know that someone is about to start pushing a herd up the trail to the railroad. No honest rancher would be gathering a herd here."

"And certainly not this time of year."

"Well, there are too many of them for us to just go driving in there. I see the cook is up now and working around the chuck wagon, so the others will soon be up too."

The eastern sky was beginning to show gray. Day was arriving and the rustlers were called by the cook. They turned out of their bedrolls and pulled on their boots. T. W. went to Sam to get the binoculars, then he began to examine the people in the camp.

Wash said, "Put your glasses on the other side of the wagon. Is that a woman lying there on the ground?"

"Good Lord, that's Penelope Copeland! And her hands are tied behind her back. Here, look."

"That's who it is, and there's somebody else over there, just climbing out of his roll. It's MacKenzie, sure enough. Here, you look."

"We've got the proof!"

"Yep. Now what do we do with it? We can't just ride up and say, 'Come with us, we're takin' you to the judge.' "

"There's also Penelope's safety to consider. Let's see what happens."

MacKenzie walked over to the chuck wagon and returned with a plate of biscuits and beef, and a cup of coffee. He set them on the ground, went behind Penelope, and untied her. She sat up, rubbing her wrists. Britt offered her the food and coffee, but she lifted her head defiantly and turned away. Britt then sat cross-legged and ate slowly. Occasionally he said something to her, but she never spoke.

"Wash, somehow she must have found out about MacKenzie and he's had to make her a prisoner."

"Yeah, he'll do away with her somewhere on the trail, run the herd over her grave, and nobody will ever know what happened to her."

"He'll put on one of the greatest acts of mourning ever seen and everyone will feel so sorry for him. Wash, I'm surprised that these men will allow him to do what he's doing and they must know that eventually he's going to kill her."

"Ordinary cowpunchers wouldn't stand for it, but these men have sunk as low as a man can sink."

Wash put the glasses on the others sitting around the fire. "I see Slim and Britt's two-gun desperado we captured a couple of weeks ago. I don't know the others. None of 'em are regular Pothook hands."

Two of the men saddled their horses and went to relieve the night watch. T. W. did not know the first one to come in, but the second one was Big John Oates.

Wash said, "There's a friend of yours, and I'm kind of surprised to see him involved in this, even though he's been punchin' cows for Britt ever since Britt came in to the valley."

"I agree. I didn't think he was the type for this kind of thing."

T. W. and Wash watched MacKenzie pull Penelope roughly to her feet and tie her hands behind her again with a pigging string. He was talking to her, but she did not look at him. She stood erect, her shoulders back and her head held high. Her hair was unkempt, streaming across her shoulders and down her back. He pushed her toward her horse. She stumbled and nearly fell but regained her balance. When Britt started to put her on her horse, she kicked at him. He easily avoided the attempt and pushed her so hard she fell heavily to the ground. He stepped toward her to kick her. T. W. jumped up, but Wash pulled him back down.

"Don't be a fool! We can't do anything yet. We'll settle with him later. Right now you'd just get yourself shot full of holes. Anyway, watch Big John."

Oates had just stepped between Britt and Penelope. He was saying something to Britt. Britt put his hand on his pistol and Big John seemed to dare him to pull it. But Britt suddenly turned away and Big John helped Penelope to her feet and then into the saddle.

MacKenzie started giving orders and the men soon had the cattle headed north.

The first day was always the toughest because the men had to break the herd to the trail. They were kept busy chasing mavericks that did not want to follow along with the rest. But MacKenzie's men were experienced and they rode good mounts. One of the men started the horse remuda, and within an hour the cattle were strung out and on their way. Britt was leading Penelope's horse and they were out in front of the herd, increasing the distance between them and the lead cattle. Big John had been assigned to ride drag. Not only was that the dirtiest, dustiest job, but it would put him so far back he could not keep tabs on what Britt was doing.

The swing riders and those on the flanks were constantly busy, chousing the mavericks back into the herd. "You know, Wash, when all this is over I'd like to go north with a herd someday."

"It's something you'd never forget. But by the time the JL drives a herd up to the railroad this fall you'll be back in Boston."

"I suppose so." Then after some thought, T. W. said, "They seem to be ignoring the possibility that we might be here. I can't understand that. Also, Britt hasn't sent anyone back to check on those men we left back on the mountain."

"As far as those killers are concerned, probably no one cares one way or another, except that MacKenzie must have been countin' on them to help with this drive. He'll probably send for some more Pothook punchers to join him."

"How about us? Slim certainly told him what happened."

"First things first, I guess. He had to get the herd on its way. There's little grass left down there. And he might have sent somebody back to the Pothook last night when Slim told him what happened."

"So there could be more men coming over the mountain right now?"

"Yep. He's got lots of 'em."

"Well, we'd better move along up here and watch Britt. Maybe we'll get a chance to rescue Penelope. Before any reinforcements arrive."

The JL men moved on, staying out of sight. The going was slow, but they made far better time than the men moving the cattle, and they had no trouble keeping up with Britt because Penelope's horse was not used to being led and resisted the constant forward pull. But there was no chance to charge in to the rescue. There was too much open ground to provide any kind of cover.

"Wash, is there another pass over the mountain?"

"Farther north? Yeah, about ten miles. Then there isn't one for fifty miles. It's the easiest of the three in this area."

"All right. Here's the plan. I know we can't handle this whole thing by ourselves."

"That's the smartest thing you've said today."

"So, you ride back and get Magruder and all of our men you can find on such short notice. Send a message to the marshal in Santa Fe to cut through the pass and intercept. In the meantime, I'll keep an eye on MacKenzie. I notice he hasn't opened up much distance between himself and the herd, so he must not be planning to do anything to Penelope this morning."

"Good plan, T. W. But you go get Magruder and I'll keep an eye on things here."

"I don't know the way back to the JL, so there's no use to argue about who goes. I could find my way back, but it would take me a lot longer."

"I don't like it, but I guess you're right. By the time I get back it'll be nearly dark and they'll have bedded down the herd. They should be close to the pass by then."

"You don't have any time to waste, old friend."

"I'm goin'. Don't do anything foolish, T. W. Just keep an eye on MacKenzie."

Wash was quickly out of sight and out of hearing. The herd moved slowly. Sometimes one longhorn would break away; sometimes ten or more would follow the first one. Each time it took a while to get them back in line. The chuck wagon passed the herd about a half mile east—out of the dust and far enough away so as not to excite the cattle.

Around noon Britt signaled the cook, who stopped and began setting up to cook a quick meal. The point man and the swing men turned the lead cattle, which began to browse. The others were driven up, and Big John stopped pushing the last ones. He and Slim stayed out with the herd while the others ate. MacKenzie did not offer Penelope any food nor help her to dismount, so she sat on horseback in the broiling midday sun.

When Big John was relieved of duty, he went to the cook and got two plates of food. He took one to Penelope and said something to her. She nodded her head and he helped her to the ground. He untied her hands, handed her the plate, and went for coffee. As far as T. W. could tell there was no conversation as they ate. When they had eaten, Big John took the plates and cups to the wagon and dropped them in the dishpan.

Shortly after, Britt gave the signal to move. While the other men saddled fresh horses the wrangler brought up, Big John tied Penelope's wrists loosely behind her and helped her into the saddle, then went about his job of riding drag. The cook started washing dishes and pans and the wrangler moved the tired remuda out to the east before turning north. Britt again began leading Penelope's horse.

T. W. ate the last of his hardtack and jerky and started north too, keeping out of sight. He soon realized that MacKenzie was pushing harder than he had in the morning. He was opening more space between himself and the herd. The pace was harder on Penelope, with her hands tied behind her. Sometimes Britt trotted the horses and that was especially tortuous for her. T. W. saw that Britt now had the cook's short-handled shovel tied behind the saddle.

He and Wash had miscalculated about Britt's plans. He was going to get rid of Penelope that afternoon, so he had to get several miles out in front in order to have enough time to shoot her, dig a shallow grave, and fill it before the cattle came along to trample over it.

T. W. had to do something. He moved Sam as fast as he could. He had to get ahead of Britt and find an arroyo that ran across the trail, toward the Pecos. He reached a dry watercourse deep enough to keep him from MacKenzie's sight as he rode out into the plain. He walked Sam so there would be no dust to give him away. When he thought he was directly in MacKenzie's path, he stopped Sam. T. W. took off his hat and crept up to the rim to see if he had figured correctly. MacKenzie was coming straight toward him, but did not see him because he had his head turned, saying something to Penelope. T. W. ran back and mounted Sam. He drew his Peacemaker.

MacKenzie came over the rim, still talking to Penelope. T. W. heard him say, "It's too bad things turned out this way. If you had minded your own business you could have married the wealthiest, most influential man in the territory."

"Stop right there, Britt. Put up your hands. Quick!"

MacKenzie tried to pull Penelope's horse between him and T. W., but Penelope kneed her horse hard in the other direction. He wheeled around behind her and spurred his horse back up the slope. T. W. fired but Sam was prancing in his excitement and the shot missed. He let MacKenzie get away—the most important thing was getting Penelope out of immediate danger. He rode over to her. She was crying. He quickly cut the pigging string around her wrists and said, "Can you ride?"

She moved her arms around in front of her and she tried to mask the pain. "Yes. He'll be back with some more of his rotten crew."

"Let's move quickly, up onto the slopes. We'll find a place for defense." Her expression seemed to say What's the use? He tried to reassure her. "Help will be coming soon. Wash has gone to get JL men and the Santa Fe marshal."

Her face was dusty, streaked with small rivulets of tears. Her hair was in disarray. Her riding costume was dirty and wrinkled. She had been humiliated and mistreated. But suddenly her head came up. There were no more tears welling from her green eyes. A fierce light replaced them. She said, "I'm ready."

T. W. handed her reins to her and they put their horses into a quick gallop. She had no trouble keeping pace with him. Back at the end of the arroyo, T. W. turned north, up into the piñons. They had to walk their horses as they searched for a place to defend themselves. Below, Mac-Kenzie had stopped the herd and was coming fast with four of his men. The others were still with the cattle. They had to find a place where they could hold off an attack, had to find at least minimal protection.

T. W. saw a place high up the slope. Some big rocks had broken off and fallen partway down. Behind them was a high bluff that ran along for two hundred yards. No one could attack from the rear or from above. The rocks were big enough to protect Penelope and him and the horses.

T. W. led the way behind the rocks and tied the horses to a piñon. Britt and five of his men were at the foot of the slope. They were planning their attack.

CHAPTER 17

"CAN YOU SHOOT, Penelope?"

"Not really well, but I've done some."

He handed his Peacemaker to her, then took two boxes of cartridges from his saddlebag, ammunition for both his Winchester and the Colt. When he had bought them at the Mercantile he had no idea how important they were going to be in his life.

Britt and his men had left their horses and were deploying in an extended line with about twenty-five yards between them. Somehow T. W. had to make their advance up the slope a time-consuming one. He had to keep them from making a concentrated rush on the rock defenses.

"They're too far for a pistol, Penelope, so save your ammunition until they get closer. I'll try to slow them up. If I can hit one, they won't take so many chances and it will give us more time."

Britt and his men were already darting from one tree or large rock to another. T. W. looked for a good target, but he never knew which man was going to move next, so he picked one and stayed with him until the next move. Several others moved from one place to another, but T. W. kept his sights on a rock where he knew one of them was. The man suddenly came out, running low. T. W. allowed for shooting downhill and squeezed off a shot. He missed his mark, but hit a rock about a foot in front of the man, who turned back to get behind the rock he had left.

T. W. quickly took cover behind another rock and a bullet ricocheted off the rock where he had been. He had to hit one of them down below there to slow them up early in their advance. He watched a rock where he had seen another man hide. T. W. decided the rustler would head for a certain rock ten feet closer, and when he exposed himself T. W. fired. The man stumbled and fell. He did not move again. The odds were now four to one, not counting Penelope.

He looked over at Penelope. She had the pistol and was peering around the edge of a boulder. Before he could say anything she aimed, fired, and pulled back her head. A bullet slammed into the bluff above her.

She said, "I thought they should know I can shoot too."

"Good idea, but shoot from a different place next time."

Wash Carter rode into JL headquarters just as some of the men were coming out of the mess hall. When they saw him slide his lathered horse to a stop in front of them, they stopped picking their teeth and watched in amazement. Wash never abused a horse and this one had been ridden hard.

He shouted, "Where's Magruder?"

Magruder stepped out of the door and said, "Here! What's happened?"

"Drop everything, Jim. We've got proof that MacKenzie is doin' the rustlin' and he's startin' a herd north right now. He's captured Penelope Copeland, got her tied up, takin' her along with the herd up to now, but he's sure goin' to kill her, and T. W. is goin' to try to stop him all by himself if we don't get there in time to help him."

Magruder ordered, "Saddle up, everybody! Fresh horses. Shorty, saddle one for Wash. Wash, get a cup of coffee and eat something while we get ready."

"Jim, T. W. said to send for the marshal and tell him he'll need a posse if he can get one together in a hurry. I think we can handle things until he gets there."

"Curly, you ride to Santa Fe. Be sure the marshal knows how serious things are and that he needs to ride hard."

Within minutes the JL crew rode out. Each man wore a six-shooter on his hip, had a rifle in his saddle scabbard and plenty of ammunition for both. The men knew they were riding into danger and might not return. Not one of them questioned whether he should go. Aside from their loyalty to Thad Love, their employer, they had come to like and respect T. W. The college boy had become one of them in a few short weeks. They were riding to his rescue and to the rescue of a woman they all held in high esteem.

Every man wanted to stretch his horse's endurance to the very limit, but they all knew there were many miles to go and the speed had to be paced or their mounts would not be able to get up and over the pass. Wash and Magruder led the way and Wash told Magruder the bare-bones story of what had happened during the past twenty-four hours.

Wash tried to estimate how far along MacKenzie would have been likely to push his rustled herd so they could intercept them with a minimum of lost minutes. He knew very well that MacKenzie might not follow the plan that Wash and T. W. had thought he most probably would. Britt might do away with Penelope at any time and when T. W. saw it about to happen, he would brave any odds to save her.

Another worry for Wash and Magruder was whether Curly had been successful in getting the marshal in Santa Fe to form a posse and ride. Even so, they probably couldn't get there in time to help with a rescue of Penelope, but the JL men would need reinforcements to defeat the fake Comancheros. Britt had a formidable small army of hired guns. If the marshal and his men arrived to help, the JL men could turn the herd and drive it back to the Estancia Valley. Later, the ranchers would be able to come and claim their own cows.

★ ★ ★

Curly reached Santa Fe and Marshal Max Bradford quickly formed a posse made up of some store owners, a lawyer, a dentist and young Doctor Parker who always kept a saddle-bag equipped with emergency supplies and instruments. He usually went with the posses in case there might be some casualties. Several cattlemen who happened to be in Santa Fe on business immediately volunteered when they heard what was happening. The town's citizens were men Bradford had counted upon in other crises.

They all gathered in the plaza and then raised a lot of dust as they rode east down Palace Avenue toward the Sangre de Cristo mountains with Curly and the marshal in the vanguard. Curly told as much about the situation as he knew and Max Bradford was happy that at last he had a chance to put a stop to the large scale rustling that had been plaguing him and the valley's ranchers.

T. W. Love had no way of knowing whether help would arrive in time. He was beginning to doubt it. The outlaw rifles would be coming closer and closer. He wanted to go on the offensive, but he couldn't leave Penelope. They really had him pinned down and there was no cover of darkness to help him this time. At least for the time being he would have to stay where he was, keep shooting and keep moving. He lay on his belly and peered around a boulder, from a low position. He picked out another rock to concentrate on, hoping someone was behind it. No one moved—anywhere. Even after several minutes there was no movement. Why had they stopped? He had hit only one. He couldn't believe he had stopped a desperate Britt so easily.

Then he saw what was happening. There was a fleeting glimpse of a figure moving low and fast, far off to the north and still downslope, maybe a hundred and fifty yards away. They had abandoned the frontal assault, in favor of flanking them. T. W. scanned the area to the south. There too, a man moved from one place to another. T. W. fired a shot, just to let the outlaw know he had seen him. There would be one or two down in front too, to make him divide his attention, but the main effort was going to be the flanking maneuver. He explained to Penelope what was happening and told her to shoot once in a while at the one to the south just to slow him up some.

There was a rifle shot from the south, but no bullet hit near them or whined off above them. It could not have come from the flanker because it was too far downslope. Had someone come to help? Wash and the JL crew could not be back yet.

Britt had seen who it was and shouted, "Oates, what the hell are you doing? Get back to the cattle. Now!"

T. W. heard John's answer: "I didn't know you were a woman killer—or a man killer. I didn't bargain for murder, so I just came over here to even the odds a little."

"I'm not telling you again, Oates. Get out of here!"

"Too late, Britt. I'm in this all the way. I already shot Slim over here, so it's just three rifles against two now."

MacKenzie suddenly exposed himself and aimed a shot at where he thought Big John was, but the big man laughed loudly and shouted, "Not even close, Britt."

Either John had not known what kind of an operation he had gotten himself into, or he had been willing to try rustling but could not accept Britt's cruelty to Penelope or this plan to murder two people.

T. W. saw some movement from the north flank and quickly turned to look. He saw a rifle spurt flame. A slug smashed into his left side. He threw his Winchester to his shoulder and fired at the crouching figure. The bullet hit the outlaw in the chest and he fell backward.

Penelope saw the blood on T. W.'s shirt and the grimace on his face. "We have to take off your shirt. Don't move. I'll do it." She assessed the extent of the wound.

T. W. forced a tight smile. "Well, what do you think, Doctor?"

"I've never seen a bullet wound before, but it looks like the bullet grazed your ribs and caromed off. I don't see a puncture wound."

Nearby, Big John continued to exchange gunfire with the rustlers.

"I think I have a rib or two broken. It really hurts when I breathe and that's the way it was once with a rugby injury."

"I'd better try to stop the bleeding." She tore off the bottom of her petticoat and ripped it into strips. Penelope placed short strips of the white cotton across the open wound, then wrapped the long pieces around his chest to keep the strips in place.

"Pull those long ones as tight as you can," he told her. "It helps keep the broken ribs from shifting around when I move. That's what the doctor in Cambridge did."

When she had tied the last knot, T. W. asked, "Do you know how to load a rifle?"

"Yes, sometimes I work in the gun section."

"Please load my Winchester, and how about the revolver?"

"I've reloaded."

"There are two left down there, aren't there?"

"Britt and another one."

There were two shots from downslope and then two more, but the bullets did not come toward Penelope and T. W. He worked his way to where he could peer around the boulder. "There they go," he said, "down the hill. They drove Big John to cover and now they're running to their horses. They're headed back to the herd."

"Think Britt's leaving?"

"He really can't. He has to get rid of us, so he must be going for reinforcements."

"Here comes John Oates. He got his horse and he's riding up here."

"We've got to move north, Penelope. I'm hoping for help coming across that pass. We should get as close to there as we can."

"But you can't ride. You can hardly stand up."

"I've got to . . ."

Big John rode in and T. W. told him how glad he was to have his help, that Wash was coming across the pass with JL men, and the marshal had been summoned from Santa Fe. He asked, "Did Britt send for more gunmen last night when Slim came in without the other three?"

"Yeah, right away. They may be back at the camp by now."

"Then we've got to move quickly."

Big John brought Sam and helped T. W. into the saddle. The three of them made their way down to the valley and started north at a gallop. T. W. had to hold on to the horn with both hands despite the pain from the deep crease on his forearm. He feared he might black out and fall from the saddle because of the intense pain from his broken ribs every time he breathed and especially when Sam's rhythm was altered because of the rough terrain. Once T. W. turned to look back, but the twisting brought whirling, exploding lights and he nearly fell from the saddle. Big John saw what happened.

"T. W., I'll keep track of things in back. You just hold on." After two more miles, John said, "They're comin' now, but they're a long ways back."

"How many?" T. W. asked.

"Looks like six besides Britt."

"Can we make it to the pass?"

"No, they're comin' hard."

"Is there a cave or some other defensive position we can get to?"

"About a mile farther. Can you make it?"

"I'll make it. But if anything happens to me, John, take care of Penelope."

After what seemed like an eternity, Big John said, "Here we are. I'll help you off. The cave ain't real big but it will hold us and the horses too. Britt can't get at us except straight on."

T. W. said, "It would be a real stronghold if we had some rocks in front of it."

John said, "I'll get us some."

In a few minutes he had pushed and rolled boulders into position, boulders few other men could have moved.

He said, "Now let 'em come." Then he frowned and asked, "We got any cartridges?"

"Some forty-four forties and some forty-fives."

"Well, we both got Winchester 'seventy-threes. It'll cost 'em to come up this hill."

When Britt and his men arrived, they dismounted and held council out of rifle range. Then they started the same pattern of attack Britt had used before. Scatter, move from vantage point to vantage point, move at irregular intervals, and not all at the same time. They did not shoot. They just kept coming closer. Before long they would be within the range of the '73s, but not their effective range.

T. W. asked, "John, think we could hit one of them yet?"

"I'll try the next one that moves."

"I found out I did better by spotting one and keeping an eye on him, then shooting on his next move."

"Sounds good. I'll try it."

In a few minutes John fired and said, "Got him in the leg. He can still shoot, but he won't be comin' any closer."

T. W. fired at a furtive figure, but missed. He stayed with his man and missed him again, but it was close enough to send him back to cover. Now the attackers began to fire at the defenders. Each man down the slope shot whenever he obtained a new position. Bullets ricocheted off the rocks John had positioned and off the roof of the cave.

Britt must be trying to kill the horses with the cave-roof shots.

Neither John nor T. W. could get a good shot. There were too many trees and rocks. And every time T. W. fired, the Winchester's kick sent an excruciating stab into his ribs.

Penelope was watching him once when he fired off a shot, saw him waver, and almost fall. She said, "T. W., give me the rifle. You've got to stop shooting." There was compassion in her voice and in her eyes.

"Thank you, Penelope, but I'm the better shot. We just have to hold them a while longer until Wash gets here with the JL men."

Penelope had reloaded the Winchester and the Peacemaker while they talked. T. W. watched her go back to her position, ready to shoot as soon as any outlaw came within pistol range. This woman was strong and courageous, refusing to give in to fear and panic. T. W. might have guessed she would be like that, as he remembered how aloof and dispassionate she had been at the store, or how commanding she had been when directing the choir. But now T. W. had seen her tenderness, her unselfish concern for others. Suddenly he knew this woman was a true Western woman—strong, ready to meet what life presented, yet tender and sensitive when life permitted that luxury.

T. W. looked down the slope. If they did not put some more outlaws out of action, they would be overrun. Wash and the JL men would be too late.

CHAPTER 18

THE SUN WAS close to the top of the mountains now. T. W. focused on a rock with a rustler behind it, waiting for him to make his next move.

"John, we've got to get a couple of them soon," T. W. said.

"You're right, pardner. I've got one behind a rock and the next time he moves he's got to cover some open space."

T. W. concentrated on his target rock. A bullet from below sent rock fragments all around him. When the man emerged, T. W. fired, his most carefully aimed shot so far. The recoil sent such pain surging through his side that he fell against the rock and did not see whether he had hit his mark. Penelope fired a shot, but Big John's gun was silent.

T. W. looked over at John. He was sitting down with his back against a rock, motionless. His eyes were closed and blood streamed from his forehead.

"John!"

No answer. T. W. crawled to him and examined his wound. A rock fragment had smashed into his forehead. His pulse was strong, but the giant was unconscious.

"Penelope, I think you'd better come over here and bandage John's head. He's alive but unconscious."

T. W. had no hope now of holding off MacKenzie's gunmen, but he was holding one card that Britt did not know about. It was an ace, too. If he could persuade Britt to accept the challenge, he felt he could beat him in a quick-draw showdown. He just had to get Britt to face him, one man against one man. It was the last chance.

Penelope had just finished tying the bandage on Big John's head. He motioned for her to come closer.

"Our only chance now is for me to lure Britt into a one-against-one confrontation."

"You can't do that, T. W. Britt has handled guns for years."

"I've practiced a lot and I'm sure I can beat Britt. If I do, his men will desert him because they won't fight without getting paid to do it."

"T. W., you just can't . . ."

"It's our only chance, Penelope."

Penelope straightened her shoulders and lifted her head. "If you say you can do it, then I believe you."

T. W. turned and shouted, "Britt, listen to me." No answer. T. W. shouted two more times.

Finally Britt answered, "What do you want, Love?"

"You've lost some men and the rest don't want to die. I hear you're fast with a gun, or at least you used to be before you hired gunslingers to do your fighting for you."

"Say what you've got to say."

"All right. I'll come out and you come out. Just you and I. Let's settle this man to man."

Britt laughed, "The three of you are as good as dead. Why should I come out?"

"You're not thinking, Britt. Your men know that at least a couple more of them are going to die before you can take us, if you ever do get us. We can shoot and they know it now. They just don't know how many more and which ones are going to die and have their bones picked clean by buzzards tomorrow."

"You're crazy, Love."

"Maybe, but you're a coward, Britt. I know it, and now your men will know it if you refuse to face me."

MacKenzie did not reply.

"Your hired guns might not want to work for a man

who's afraid of a shootout with a city dude. You've got some of them right there with you. Ask them, Britt."

"All right, damn you. I'll count to three and we both step out."

"Just you and I, Britt. Keep your men out of this."

T. W. loosened the Peacemaker in his holster. He could not trust MacKenzie. The man had absolutely no sense of honor, so he planned to draw as soon as he was close enough and had a clear shot. It was unlikely the gunslingers would let this be a fair fight because it was in their interest to keep Britt alive so they would still draw their pay. T. W. heard MacKenzie count to three and he stepped into the open. They were too far apart for revolver accuracy. MacKenzie stood his ground, but T. W. started down the slope. . . .

Wash, Magruder, and seven other JL men had entered the area from the pass and had heard the shooting. They dismounted and were approaching through the trees when T. W. and MacKenzie stepped out. They stopped short when they saw what was happening. They were within accurate rifle distance, but Magruder said, "Quiet! We can't distract him. Everybody pick an outlaw and shoot him if it looks like he's going to deal himself into this."

Big John Oates was still unconscious, but Penelope Copeland saw the JL men. She knew she could not call to them. She could only watch the drama unfold.

T. W. picked his way carefully. He had to focus on MacKenzie, knowing that Britt would take advantage of any T. W. misstep, any stumble, any unbalanced position. The only advantage T. W. had was that Britt did not know how fast he was. Britt had every other advantage.

T. W. would go on the offense, a few more steps and he would draw, shoot MacKenzie, throw himself on the ground. If the shock of pain did not cause him to black out, he would roll and present a moving target to any outlaw who might be shooting at him. Then he would try to return the fire.

Britt MacKenzie saw coming slowly toward him what almost appeared to be an apparition. Bareheaded and bare to the waist, a bloody forearm, a large, white, bloodied bandage around his chest, the specter came on. The eyes burned with intensity and iron will. For the first time MacKenzie's face showed doubt.

T. W. moved past one more piñon and his hand streaked for his gun. MacKenzie's face registered surprise. His gun was only half out of the holster when the big slug tore into his body and sent him reeling backward. T. W. threw himself to the ground and guns exploded all around him. The pain sent flashes and pinwheels of light bursting instantaneously in his head, then merciful black nothingness engulfed him.

Words were coming from far away, a woman's words. They were spoken softly, gently urging him to open his eyes. They seemed to be coming closer and he tried to force himself back to reality. He heard his name and when he opened his eyes, he was looking into concerned green ones. Penelope was holding his head tenderly and she said, "Everything is all right. Everything is all right."

T. W. compelled himself to examine his surroundings. He saw Wash, who said, "It's about time you woke up. I knew I shouldn't have left you alone. Looks like I spend most of my time gettin' you out of one scrape after another."

T. W. smiled, then he saw Duke, Brick, Shorty, the other JL men, and Big John Oates. T. W. asked, "Where's Jim Magruder?"

Wash answered, "He's dead. He led this rescue party. One of MacKenzie's thugs shot him during the skirmish."

"I'm really sorry, Wash."

Penelope said quietly, "You need to rest. You can find out about everything soon."

T. W. looked up at her, "How about Britt?"

"He's going to live—to stand trial for his crimes."

"Good news, good news," T. W. whispered as he sank back into sleep.

A week later T. W. wrote to Thad Love, telling him the whole story and how they had buried Jim Magruder up on the ridge north of the house, with a stone marker and a fence to keep the cattle off the grave. Then he wrote:

I hope you will not be too disappointed when I tell you that I do not want to be a Boston banker. I want to live in this high New Mexico country. It is far from the artificiality of the eastern cities. And I have found a woman whom I want to "ride the river" with. Her name is Penelope Copeland.

T. W. explained how he would like to manage the JL, with Washington Carter as his foreman. If Thad did not approve of the idea, then T. W. would ask to use his trust fund to start a ranch of his own.

Two weeks later Thad's reply arrived, expressing sorrow about Magruder's untimely death, and explaining how he had sold Magruder a partial partnership in the JL. He included the address of Jim's sister, who was Jim's legal heir.

T. W. rode into Yucca to share the letter with Penelope, especially the last paragraph:

. . . and I had hoped you would love the West. I have deeded the JL to you. Your father and mother would be happy to know their son is the owner of the John Love ranch. But I hope I can lay claim to a room for a few weeks in October each year, when the Sangre de Cristo mountains are covered with the gold of the aspen leaves. That is, if Penelope can put up with an old codger who still loves the JL and the high Estancia valley.

T. W. mounted Sam and started down the main street. He saw Jennifer Prentice walking toward the Mercantile, holding a pretty parasol over her head. Gallantly, he doffed his hat, smiled broadly, and said, "Good afternoon, Miss Prentice."

With a genuinely warm smile, she answered, "Good afternoon, Mr. Love."

As T. W. rode by the hotel, he saw Big John and his sidekick Sundown lolling on the veranda. "Howdy, men."

Big John answered and waved, then he said, "Sundown, say howdy. Now there's a real man."

If you have enjoyed this book and would like to receive details about other Walker Western titles, please write to:

Western Editor
Walker and Company
720 Fifth Avenue
New York, NY 10019